HIS TO PROTECT

ELITE FORCE SECURITY

CHRISTINA TETREAULT

His To Protect, ©2019 by Christina Tetreault
Published by Christina Tetreault
Cover Designer: Amanda Walker
Photographer: CJC Photography
Cover Model: Jered Youngblood
Editing: Hot Tree Editing

Digital ISBN: **978-1-7329429-4-3**

Print ISBN: 978-1-7329429-5-0

ONE

Thump. Thump. The sound of boxing gloves hitting a bag filled the air as Gabriel Wilson walked across the training floor and toward the stairwell. He'd spent much of his life in gyms similar to this one and barely registered the sounds or the smell of sweat anymore. Opening the door, he headed downstairs. At one time, the gym, located in a refurbished mill building, had only occupied the ground floor. When his brother invited him to become a partner, they'd expanded, and now it encompassed two. Upstairs, where he tended to stay, was designed for those serious about boxing, wrestling, and MMA fighting. However, the first floor was the area that brought in the real money. It was amazing how many people signed contracts for gym memberships, used them for a few months, and then never came back despite the fees they dished out every month.

He passed by the glass wall. On the other side of it, he saw the gym's indoor pools. At the moment, the slide into the family section was open and children of various ages waited in line for a turn while others swam. Across the way in the lap pool, swim lessons were underway in the first three lanes, while members swam laps in the last two. In the lane closest to the window, a girl about eleven or twelve years old positioned herself on the starting block and listened to the swim instructor in the water.

It's not Ava. Gabe clenched his fists and forced his gaze forward. For the moment, he needed to remain in control. After his meeting, he could go upstairs and beat the shit out of a bag or get in the ring with someone. He didn't care which, as long as his fist made contact with something.

Gabe nodded in his younger brother's direction as he passed Xander's open office door. While the second floor and the serious training remained his domain, Xander took care of the day-to-day operations of the gym he'd opened while Gabe was still in prison. Xander was also the guy people went to when they wanted to complain. Unlike him, his brother had the patience for other people's bullshit.

Entering his own office, he closed the door and sat behind his desk. He knew he shouldn't do it. Looking at the picture would only fuel his rage, but he couldn't stop himself from opening the desk drawer and pulling out the framed photo. In it, Ava, Logan, and his ex-wife, Savannah, smiled back at him with the Pacific Ocean and Diamond Head behind them. He remembered the moment he'd snapped the picture during their last family vacation seven months before his life went to hell.

A knock on the door ripped him away from the pleasant memory. Dropping the frame into the drawer, he slammed it closed. "Yeah."

The door opened, and an employee who worked the front desk stuck his head inside the room. "Gabe, there's a guy here who says he has an appointment with you."

He was only expecting one person this afternoon, and he was right on time. "Tell him to come in."

The employee pushed the door open more, and his

appointment entered the room. Dressed in black cargo pants and a gray T-shirt, nothing about the man stood out. If someone passed by him on the street, no one would ever remember anything specific about him. Except perhaps his hefty price tag, but according to Zane, a guy Gabe had trained regularly until his recent arrest, the former Green Beret was not only good but also discreet and willing to bend the rules to get the job done. Even better, he didn't care why you hired him or what you intended to do with the information he provided to you, as long as he got paid when the job was done.

"Sam Nixon," the private investigator said, extending his hand toward Gabe.

Shaking his hand, Gabe gestured to the chair opposite his desk. "Gabe Wilson. Have a seat." Before he sat down again, he walked around his desk and closed the office door. The gym was a noisy place, but he wasn't taking any chances someone would walk by and overhear their conversation.

Sam waited until Gabe sat down at his desk before speaking again. "On the phone, you said you needed help finding someone."

Tapping his fingertips against each other, he nodded. "Yeah. In high school, there was a guy who helped with the wrestling team my senior year. He knew my foster parents were assholes, and I think he felt sorry for me. He used to invite me over for the holidays and stuff. We stayed in contact for about a year after I graduated. Then I left the area. I've been trying to track him down for a couple of years, but I haven't had any luck. He doesn't know it, but it's because of him I'm where I am today. I'd like to thank him and his family."

Gabe had no problem with lying, but it'd taken him some time to come up with a plausible bullshit story to give Sam today. The private investigator had worked for criminals like

Zane in the past, so Gabe wasn't too worried the dude would say anything to the authorities if he later learned Armstrong went missing. Regardless, he saw no reason to share his true reasons with the guy either.

"Should be doable. What's the guy's name?" Sam pulled a small notebook and a pen from one of his pockets.

Gabe tensed the muscles in his forearm and clenched his jaw. "Edward Armstrong."

"Any idea how old he'd be now?"

"Late fifties, early sixties."

"You said he had a family. What's his wife's name?"

"Don't know. When I saw her, I called her Mrs. Armstrong."

"Was he a teacher at the high school?"

"No. He was an FBI agent. I think he was friends with the coach or maybe the principal, and that was why he helped out."

Sam jotted his answers down in the notebook and looked back up at him. "Do you know what field office he worked out of?"

Gabe knew damn well the answer to that question. "Norfolk."

The private detective shot off several more questions. Many of them Gabe could answer. When he said he didn't know, Sam didn't blink an eye. At least until he asked about the last address Gabe had for Armstrong.

Sam narrowed his eyes. "You celebrated holidays with the guy and his wife but don't remember his address at the time?"

When he'd done his own brief internet search, he'd found several people named Edward Armstrong living in and around the Norfolk area as well as other parts of Virginia. He had no way of knowing if any of them were the guy he wanted. If he gave the private detective any of the addresses, it might send him after the wrong person, wasting a lot of time and Gabe's money. He'd already lost enough thanks to Edward Armstrong. He didn't intend to lose anything else.

"I went to their house three or four times, and it was more than twenty-five years ago. Would you remember the address?"

The private detective shrugged, but his expression didn't change. "Maybe. Maybe not." Sam's tone told him the guy wasn't buying Gabe's story. "Listen, I don't care what your reasons are for tracking down this guy. But the more info I have, the easier it'll be for me and the sooner you'll have his location."

"Like I said, it's because of him I'm where I am today. I just want to repay the favor." Something he'd been waiting four long years to do.

Sam shoved the notebook back in his pocket and stood up. "I'll be in touch when I have something. You've got my number. If you think of anything else that might be useful, call me."

When the door closed behind the private investigate, Gabe yanked the desk drawer open and pulled out first the photo and then the bottle of scotch he kept under it. He didn't bother with a glass. His eyes settled on the family photo as he removed the stopper, and he took a swig. The smoky liquid burned its way down his throat and to his belly.

He didn't doubt Sam would track down Armstrong, his wife, and any children. Once Gabe had that information, he could proceed with his plan. Soon he'd destroy Special Agent Armstrong's life the same way he'd ruined his. Gabe took another hit from the bottle and returned it and the photo. Then he headed back upstairs ready for a good fight.

TWO

"How's Hot Buns?"

The coffee sprayed from Kenzie's mouth all over the kitchen table and the bagel on her plate. Grabbing a paper towel, she wiped the liquid up while she tried to get her coughing under control. "Where do you come up with these things?"

"Oh, please, there's no way you haven't noticed his ass by now," her cousin said.

Of course she had, but still, Hot Buns? It was worse than the first nickname Megan gave him when she came to visit several months ago. And she'd thought Mr. Too-Yummy-For-Words was a terrible moniker, even if it was an appropriate description. When it came to her next-door neighbor, the man was the total package, and that included his personality, which was something she couldn't say about too many men.

Before she could agree or disagree with her cousin, Megan continued. "If I lived closer, I would've snatched him up a long time ago, cuz. I don't know why you waited so long."

Although it was unlikely Ryan would be in his backyard

this early in the morning, Kenzie glanced toward the window over the kitchen sink that provided her with a glimpse into his yard. As she expected at five o'clock in the morning, his yard was empty. "He's good. We're going out again tonight."

"Date number six in like what, two and a half weeks? Sounds like things between you and Hot Buns are getting serious fast."

Leave it to her cousin to keep track of her love life. "I'm not sure you can count the first one as a real date. He was having friends over for a cookout anyway and invited me to join them. Neighbors do things like that."

Dustin and Annabeth, the owners of the house on the other side of her, had invited her over for countless cookouts since she'd moved into the community last year. They'd also invited Ryan, who had moved in a few months after she did to a few, as well as Josh and Robby, the couple who lived across the street.

"You and Mr. Too-Yummy-For-Words have been neighbors for almost a year, and he never invited you over until a couple of weeks ago. Regardless of whether or not he had friends there, I'd put the cookout in the date category."

Kenzie wanted to argue with her cousin, but she couldn't. Sure they'd chatted whenever they were both outside, and he'd even brought Marley home the day he escaped from her yard. But in the almost twelve months they'd been neighbors, he'd never invited her to any of the parties he'd had. Of course, up until about five months ago, she'd been involved with someone. Other than Ryan's friend Maddie, she'd never seen any women coming or going from his house—not that she spied on him or anything. But she doubted Ryan lived like a monk either. In her experience, single men as handsome as him didn't spend their free time alone.

"Since you're such an expert on the subject, I'll take your word for it. But please stop with the nicknames already. If you keep referring to him as Hot Buns, next time I see him, it'll probably slip out." Even as she said the words, an image of Ryan's well-toned butt materialized. The man had one gorgeous-looking backside.

"Fine." They might be almost four thousand miles apart at the moment, but Kenzie could almost hear her cousin rolling her eyes. "What are you and Ryan doing tonight?"

Kenzie reached for the half of her bagel not coated in coffee and checked her watch. She couldn't stay on the phone too much longer. "Not sure. He made the plans this time."

After sinking her teeth into the bagel, she licked the peanut butter and chocolate hazelnut spread off her finger. Other people could keep their cream cheese or butter. She liked her toast and bagels covered with an obnoxious amount of peanut butter.

"I hope his idea of a nice night out is better than Cullen's."

Kenzie grimaced at the reminder of her ex. They'd dated for two and a half months, months of her life she could unfortunately never get back. She probably wouldn't have even stayed in the relationship that long if Cullen hadn't been her close friend's brother. The man's idea of a great date night included watching him play in his bowling league every Friday night. Nothing against bowling, because with the right group of people it could make for a fun night out occasionally, but sitting there and watching someone else play all night was boring as hell.

"Shelly has better ideas than Cullen." Kenzie's goddaughter was almost eleven, and whenever she saw her, Shelly asked her to take her either to the indoor rock climbing gym or for a hike. Regardless of which they decided on, they both always enjoyed their outings together.

Megan's laugh came through the phone loud and clear. "I

don't doubt it. I never got why you stayed with him as long as you did. Is Mr. Despot still bugging you?"

Her cousin had outgrown several habits but one she'd never given up was coming up with nicknames for people. Sometimes those names were complimentary, and other times not so much. Regardless, they were always spot-on. Cullen had been boring, but it wasn't his worst flaw. She'd put an end to their relationship because of his growing desire to control her. She was a responsible adult. She didn't need or want anyone telling her what she could or couldn't do.

"He sent me a text message about three weeks ago. But nothing since. I'm hoping he's finally given up." The man really didn't understand the meaning of "this isn't working."

"If not, you could ask Hot—" Megan paused. "—Ryan to have a little chat with him. I get the impression he can be intimidating when he wants to be."

She didn't doubt for a moment that in the right circumstance, Ryan and all his friends she'd met so far could be intimidating.

"Yikes, I didn't realize it was so late. I'm supposed to meet some coworkers in ten minutes. They're taking me into Bath for the day," Megan continued.

For the past two weeks, her cousin had been in Bristol, England, for work. To say she was a little jealous would be the understatement of the century. For several years, she'd wanted to visit Ireland again before popping over to England and Scotland and spending some time exploring both places. Unfortunately, for various reasons, the most recent being her decision to buy a new home, it just hadn't happened yet. But it was on her list of things to do within the next three years, right along with buying a convertible—something she'd wanted since before she even got her driver's license.

"Lucky." Kenzie broke off a piece of her bagel and held it out to Marley, who was nudging her leg with his nose in an annoying and somewhat endearing habit he'd developed since she adopted him.

"If you get a chance, call me tomorrow. I want to know how tonight goes. Does he know today is your birthday?"

"I never told him." And she didn't know when his birthday was either. They'd shared a lot of personal information, including where they grew up and their favorite foods, but birthdays had never come up.

"Whatever you do, have fun. Talk to you later."

Have fun? Oh, she planned to. But first, she had a day of work ahead of her. Birthday or no birthday, this weekend it was her turn in the rotation at the immediate care clinic where she worked as a physician's assistant. On the positive side, at least she had the early shift.

After ending the call, she checked her watch again. As long as she didn't linger in the shower, she had enough time for another cup of coffee before she left. And she suspected she'd need all the energy she could get today. Regardless of the day of the week, the clinic was rarely empty. But since the start of the school year, every day had been a revolving door of sick children and often their ill parents. It happened each year once students went back to the classrooms or, as she liked to think of them, life-sized petri dishes.

Thanks to the frequent lack of hot water in college, she'd perfected the art of a quick shower. So less than forty minutes after finishing her conversation with her cousin, Kenzie was hitting the button on the garage door opener.

A glance in the rearview mirror showed nothing but sunshine and the houses across the street. The sound of a tinkling sleigh bell erupted from the cell phone on the passenger seat before she put the car in reverse.

Happy Birthday. We'll see you tomorrow. The message from Mom read.

Sometimes it was a day or two before or a few days after,

but in thirty-four years not a single birthday had gone by that she hadn't seen her mom. Even when her parents were living in upstate New York and she'd been in college in Virginia, her mom had made the trip down—her father too whenever possible. And ever since her parents relocated to Virginia, neither had missed a single one.

Can't wait to see you.

While she was looking forward to the visit, she was glad her parents were the ones doing the three-hour drive up from their vacation house in Virginia Beach, where they'd been for the past week, and not her.

After tossing the phone aside, Kenzie checked the rearview mirror one more time before backing out.

Thud. She didn't need to get out of her car to know that sound meant she had a flat tire. "Just wonderful."

If she called the roadside assistance club, they'd change the tire for her—and probably in much less time than it would take her. But she knew from experience that unless you were stuck on the side of the road in the dead of the night, they took their sweet time getting out to you. She didn't have time to sit around and wait right now. This morning she'd have to handle it herself and hope she didn't get filthy in the process.

Kenzie slammed the door with far more force than necessary and glared at the back tire as she passed it. Seriously, of all days to get a flat tire, she had to get it on her birthday. Popping the trunk, she reached for the jack.

Backing out of his garage, Ryan ran through his mental to-do list. When he glimpsed Kenzie pulling a spare tire from the trunk of her car, he hit the brakes. The gym and his to-do list could wait.

"Need some help?" he called out as he crossed the lawn separating their yards.

Turning, she greeted him with a smile that got him every time. Her smile wasn't merely the curving of her lips; it somehow lit up her face and reached her eyes. Actually, it'd been one of the first things he noticed about her when they met last year. Her eyes had been the other characteristic that caught and held his attention. He'd met people on every continent, but he'd never seen anyone with eyes the color of hers. A light gray, they reminded him of the sky during a rainstorm.

"It looks like you're on your way out. I can manage."

Self-sufficient, he liked that in a woman. Not to say he didn't enjoy doing things for the people he cared about, but he liked knowing that if he wasn't around his girlfriend could handle whatever came up. Especially since he sometimes was away for days or weeks at a time.

"The gym isn't going anywhere. Neither are the dumb-bells inside. I really don't mind." And he didn't. He'd never turn down a chance to spend more time with her.

"In that case, it's all yours."

He took the spare tire from her and then grabbed the cross wrench from the trunk.

"Why do I get the impression you weren't referring to the actual dumbbells you lift but your friends?" She followed him around to the side of the car.

"Because I wasn't. Don't worry, I've heard Keith and Spike call me worse." Some of them were words he wouldn't repeat in front of her.

Grabbing the jack, he slid it under the vehicle. Once he had the car high enough, he picked up the cross wrench and attacked the lug nuts on the tire. "Is three thirty still okay for this afternoon?" Ryan glanced away from what he was doing for a moment. Today she was wearing maroon-colored scrubs. He shouldn't find the outfit sexy, but he did. And at the moment, his body was letting him know just how sexy.

She crouched down next to him and held out her hand for the lug nut he'd just removed from the tire. "Yep. But how about a clue as to what we're doing."

He knew today was her birthday. He'd noticed it on her wall calendar when he'd been over last week. Both his sisters and his mom liked surprises on their birthdays, so he was working under the assumption Kenzie did too. "Sorry, you'll have to wait."

Kenzie accepted the second lug nut and nudged his arm with her elbow. "If I don't know what you have planned, I won't know how to dress."

Naked works for me. Immediately he regretted the thought as his brain conjured up an image of Kenzie naked—or at least how he imagined she looked. "Go with shorts."

"Guess that rules out the opera or the ballet tonight."

There were still a lot of things he didn't know about her, but Kenzie didn't strike him as the opera-loving type. And the only music he'd ever heard her play while working in her yard fell into two categories: rock and country. "You're into opera?"

He'd survived his younger sister's boy band phase. But if the little he'd heard of opera was a fair representation of the music, he wasn't sure he'd ever make it through an entire production.

"Beats me. I've never listened to any." She paused and accepted the last lug nut. "Unless you count the rock opera *Tommy*. I watched it in eighth or ninth grade. I'm pretty sure Mozart's *Don Giovanni* sounds nothing like *Tommy*. Not that I've heard it performed."

He'd watched the rock opera but hadn't cared for it. "Never heard of *Don Giovanni*, but I don't think there's anything out there similar to *Tommy*."

"I can't disagree with you there. It's probably one of a kind."

Her voice contained a gentle trace of humor, and he glanced over at her in time to catch her smiling, a sight he could truly look at all day.

"You know, 'wear shorts' isn't a lot to go on. I mean, should I wear a pair of old cutoffs, biking shorts, Bermuda style? A little more information would be helpful."

Ryan pulled the flat tire off and slid the spare into place. "Wear whatever you're comfortable in. And that's all I'm telling you."

"Okay, but if you show up tonight and I have on my ratty old cutoffs, it's your fault."

He'd seen her gardening in her old cutoffs, and if she answered the door wearing them tonight, he'd have no complaints. Kenzie's legs might not be long, but they earned an A+ in his book, and the shorts she was referring to showcased them well. In fact, everything about her earned an A+ in his opinion. While Hollywood and magazines might prefer women with thighs narrower than his forearm, he preferred women who looked like they ate more than once a month. Women he didn't feel like he needed to tether to his body with a rope when it was windy out because they might blow away. Kenzie Armstrong was the perfect example of the type of woman he was attracted to. Her body suggested she worked out regularly but also enjoyed pizza and cheeseburgers.

It didn't take him long to put the lug nuts back on and lower the car to the ground. Grabbing the flat and the jack, he carried them back to the trunk.

She dropped the cross wrench inside next to the other tools and then closed the gap between them. "Thanks for taking care of that. I know how, but it would've taken me a lot longer." Her palms traveled over his biceps before settling on his shoulders.

Except for the kisses he'd given her, he'd been a good

boy and kept his hands to himself. While he never hesitated to ask a woman out, when it came to the physical aspects of a relationship, he either needed clear signs from the woman it was what she wanted or he needed her to initiate. Until this moment, the only signs he'd gotten from Kenzie were that she was open to some kissing. Not that it bothered him. Unlike others in his family, he had patience. And when it came to Kenzie, he suspected his patience would pay off.

After changing the tire, there was no way his hands were clean, but with her standing this close and her touch burning holes in his old T-shirt, not even a gun to his back could keep him from placing them on her waist and moving forward so their bodies touched. Lowering his head, he zeroed in on his target. Before he reached it, her lips touched his.

His body urged him to tease her lips apart, see what she tasted like this morning. His hands wanted to reach up and tug her hair free of the tight bun she wore so he could sink his fingers into it, find out if it was as silky as it looked.

Self-control kept him from doing either. Kenzie was a lot different from the women he'd dated recently. She wasn't the type who spent an hour drinking with him at the bar before inviting him back to her place or following him up to his hotel room.

He felt the subtle change in their kiss and knew she was ending it. It didn't matter. When Kenzie pulled her mouth away, a jolt of disappointment ripped through him. And only one thought raced through his mind: getting his lips on hers again.

"If I don't go now, I'll be late for work." Despite the statement, Kenzie's hands stayed on his shoulders and she made no move to put distance between them.

"We can't have you getting in trouble." He whispered the words near her lips before kissing her. "I'll see you later."

She finally dropped her arms to her sides and stepped back. "Looking forward to it."

Ryan waited until she backed into the street before getting into his car and heading toward the headquarters for Elite Force Security. Since the security firm needed all of its employees to stay in shape, they'd made sure to incorporate a state-of-the-art fitness center—complete with weights, cardio equipment, and a lap pool—when they'd had the new headquarters built twelve years ago. Although he could use a gym closer to where he lived, he preferred to use the facility at work and keep more money in his pocket. Most of the employees did the same, especially the other members of the Hostile Response Team or HRT, as they usually called it.

There was no such thing as zero traffic between where he lived and Elite Force in Alexandria. But some days it was not too bad, while at other times it sucked. Thanks to the fact it was a Saturday and early in the morning, Ryan pulled up to the employee entrance thirty minutes later and punched in his security code.

Except for fellow HRT member and good friend Keith Wallace, the gym was empty when Ryan walked in.

"About time you got your ass here. Spending time with your neighbor again?" Keith called out as he added weight plates to the bar on the floor.

"Hey, at least I don't have to pay to get some." Usually there was no shortage of women in Keith's life, and they both knew it. Keith's current lack of dates and sex right now was self-induced. Ryan wouldn't let the detail stop him from busting the guy's ass.

In response, Keith flipped him the bird and then got in position to knock out a set of deadlifts. Once he finished, he dropped the bar to the floor and grabbed his water. "Did you lose track of time playing doctor with your neighbor?"

Ryan selected the warm-up he wanted on the treadmill

and hit Start. "Kenzie is a physician's assistant, not a doctor. And I helped her change a tire."

Shaking his head, Keith put the water down and got into position for another set. "Damn, that means I owe Spike fifty bucks."

The door leading into the men's locker room opened before Keith finished his sentence.

"I told him you were doing things differently with your next-door neighbor, Salty," Jonathan "Spike" Brockman said as he entered the room. Perspiration already dripped down his forehead, and a ring of sweat stained his sleeveless T-shirt.

Out of everyone at Elite Force, Ryan was closest to Spike. They'd grown up together in Portsmouth, New Hampshire, and it had been Spike who gave his name to the firm's director as a potential addition to the team. And while he hung out with everyone on the team and considered them his second family, he spent the most time with Spike.

Grabbing the water bottle off a bench, Spike downed the rest of it before tossing it in the trash against the wall. "Maybe if you get some pointers from Salty, you won't find yourself alone every night, Keith."

In the process of lifting the bar, Keith sent them both a dirty look but for a change kept his trap shut.

Although clearly warmed up, Spike jumped on the treadmill next to him. "If you don't have any plans, my parents and Audrey will be here this weekend. She wants to check out Georgetown and a few other universities in the area. Stop by. They want to see you."

It didn't seem possible that Spike's youngest sister was old enough to be looking at colleges. Ryan could still remember being over at the Brockman house and agreeing to partake in tea parties. He'd eaten more cookies and drunk more water from tiny plastic teacups than any man without a daughter should be expected to.

He didn't want to commit to anything this weekend, but if they were still around next week, he'd love to see them. The Brockmans had been his second family growing up. "How long are they staying?"

His friend increased the treadmill's speed and elevation. "They're heading back sometime on Tuesday."

"I'll stop by on Monday night."

Keith grabbed two more forty-five-pound weight plates and carried them over to the bar he was using. "What's on the agenda tonight for you and the physician's assistant?"

"Heading over to a botanical garden. Afterward, I'm cooking Kenzie dinner and planning to watch the Nationals game."

"Maybe I need to give you and Keith help." Spike shook his head in disbelief. "A visit to see plants and then the baseball game at your house, really? I suggest you cook her one hell of a meal tonight."

Keith's cell phone rang just as he was adding the additional weight to one side of the bar. "I have to agree with Spike on that one." Picking up the device, he checked the caller ID. For the most part, none of them interrupted their workouts for a call unless it was from either Ax, their boss, or family. "Be right back," he said before walking toward the locker room.

Kenzie's yard was an oasis of flowers and shrubs, and he regularly saw her working in the various flowerbeds. Someone who spent that much time gardening would enjoy a visit to a botanical garden. However, a trip to Meadow Valley hadn't been his first idea for tonight. Before settling on the idea, he'd looked into getting them tickets to see the Nationals play. He knew Kenzie was a baseball fan, because she often wore a Washington Nationals baseball hat. He'd seen her wearing a sweatshirt with the team name on it as well.

Unfortunately, the team was playing out in San Diego this weekend.

"I've done my intel gathering. She's going to love what I have planned."

"Hey, it's your funeral." Spike used the bottom of his shirt to wipe the sweat off his forehead. "I cannot get my head around the fact Audrey's a senior this year. I still remember when she'd run around the house in nothing but a diaper. If she doesn't go to a school close to home, Mom and Dad hope she goes to one around here so I can keep an eye on her. Unfortunately, Tulane and USC are still her top two picks."

"I hope your parents didn't tell her that. She'll cross anything within a hundred-mile radius of you off her list." The running program ended, and Ryan grabbed his water. "If we didn't work together, I wouldn't want to be within a hundred miles of you either."

Next to him, Spike stopped running and got off his treadmill. "Keep telling yourself that. We both know the truth. You took the job here so you could be close to me." After taking a swig of water from a new bottle, he pointed it toward a bench. "Do you mind spotting me?"

Ryan didn't understand the science behind it, but he could always get in one or two extra repetitions if he had someone spotting him when he bench-pressed. He knew the same was true for others. Moving into position, he glanced at the locker room door. "Do you think he's talking to Mad Dog?"

Thanks to a few too many beers one night, it was no secret to him or Spike that Keith had it bad for Maddie Dempsey, better known as Mad Dog to the other team members. Why his buddy didn't just grow a set already and do something about it was a mystery to him.

"Doubt it. She mentioned flying to Myrtle Beach for a girls' weekend. She left sometime yesterday."

He was about to point out her current whereabouts didn't

rule out anything, when Keith walked back in the room. Ryan didn't know whom his friend had been talking to, but his expression suggested someone had told him the sun did, in fact, revolve around the Earth and scientists had been lying to the world for years.

Bench press forgotten for the moment, Spike moved into an upright position again. "Hey, is everything okay?"

"Yeah." Keith sat on the weight bench opposite them. "My sister wanted to talk."

Although he'd never met either of Keith's sisters, his friend had mentioned them. As far as Ryan knew, they both lived in Rhode Island.

Leaning forward, Keith rested his forearms on his knees and shook his head. "Jen is dating an army buddy of mine."

"Sorry, man." Thankfully, neither of his sisters ever got involved with any of his friends, but one had dated a longtime friend of his older brother. Or maybe he should say a former friend of Kyle's. After Kyle learned his buddy was cheating on their sister, both relationships ended.

"I don't care about that. Sherbrooke is a decent guy. But she's been communicating with him for two years and neither of them ever bothered to tell me."

Yeah, he'd be pissed off too if either of his sisters did that to him. "Wait a minute. Your sister is dating Brett Sherbrooke? The dude running for the open senate seat in DC? A picture of him kissing a woman in a parking garage came up on my newsfeed the other day. That was your sister?"

Ryan didn't follow politics closely, especially when it didn't involve issues in his own state. But the current special election in Massachusetts was getting nationwide attention because Brett Sherbrooke, a member of the wealthiest family in America as well as President Warren Sherbrooke's nephew, was running. When the news first broke that the guy had entered the race, Keith had admitted he knew the guy well and would vote for him if he could.

Keith shrugged. "Must have been. Jen didn't mention it."

Laughing, Ryan shook his head. "Does that mean you'll be getting an invitation to Uncle Warren's for a family dinner?"

"I think they have standards at the White House. Standards our buddy here will never meet." Spike moved back into position under the bar.

"Hey, you never know, Spike. President Sherbrooke has a dog." Ryan glanced in Keith's direction. "If they'll let a four-legged animal into the White House, I think there's a decent chance they'll let you in. Don't give up hope just yet."

Keith didn't waste the energy it would take to respond. Instead, he went back to his deadlifts.

Reaching up, Spike gripped the weight bar. "What's on the menu tonight, Chef?"

THREE

Dragging a brush through her hair, Kenzie reached for her iced coffee and took a sip. As she'd expected, there had been a nonstop stream of patients today. In fact, it'd been so busy she'd never gotten around to taking a proper lunch break. Instead, she'd downed one of the meal replacement shakes she kept in the kitchen at the clinic. Although not her preferred lunch, it kept her stomach moderately happy while she pushed through the rest of the day. Then on her way home, she'd stopped at her favorite coffee shop and grabbed an extra-large mocha-flavored iced coffee with a shot of espresso and a blueberry scone. She needed both to hold her over for a few hours. Perhaps even longer, since she didn't know what Ryan had planned.

"Should I wear my hair up or down, Marley?" Kenzie turned and looked at the dog lounging on the bed. Unless he was busy chasing birds and squirrels out of the yard, Marley made sure he was near her. He even tried to follow her into the bathroom.

At the sound of his name, the dog picked his head up.

"Yeah, I'm not sure either." It was hot this afternoon. If

Ryan's plans included time in the sun, she'd want her hair off her neck. But if they would be indoors with air-conditioning, it didn't matter much either way.

With a shrug, she pulled it back and secured it in place. She'd play it on the safe side just in case.

"C'mon, buddy. Let's go downstairs, and I'll feed you." Again Ryan's refusal to give her an itinerary meant she didn't know what time she'd be home. She'd feel awful if Marley had to wait until ten or eleven o'clock to eat dinner.

If being with her and chasing birds were his two favorite activities, eating came in at a close third. Before Kenzie moved from her spot in front of the mirror, he'd leaped from the bed and was in the hall waiting for her.

She grabbed the iced coffee and glanced at her cat, who was resting on the window seat and sunning herself. "What about you, Silver? Are you staying or coming with me?"

Unlike Marley, who would attach himself to her if he could, Silver liked to do her own thing. Sometimes she wanted attention, and she'd curl up in Kenzie's lap while she watched television or she'd sit on her feet while she ate breakfast. Other times she wanted to be left alone to sunbathe or hunt in the backyard.

This afternoon, Silver let Kenzie know which she was in the mood for. She didn't bother to lift her head at the sound of her name. From experience, Kenzie knew the cat would probably stay there until the sunlight no longer came through the window.

Downstairs, Kenzie and Marley noticed Ryan coming up the walkway at the same time. Immediately, the speed of the dog's tail accelerated, going from slow to Mach 5, and he started barking. Regardless of who came to the house, he barked. As long as it was a friend or family member, he stopped once they acknowledged him. Much like a small child, Marley didn't like it when people ignored him. It was a different story if a stranger approached the house. Then he would only quiet down if she gave the command. While the dog was the biggest sweetheart to those he knew, he looked and sounded ferocious when he got going—a fact she found reassuring. While she lived in a safe neighborhood and had vigilant neighbors, she still lived alone, and if anyone tried to enter the house that didn't belong and saw Marley, they'd think twice about proceeding.

Ryan didn't enter when she opened the door. "Hey there, buddy." He scratched the dog near his collar, and in return, Marley licked his arm as if to say hello. "It's nice to see you too." He gave the dog one last pat before crossing into the house.

"What, no scratch behind the ears for me?"

His lips curved into a devastating grin that had Kenzie wishing she had a fan handy. Then he winked, and her knees got a little wobbly. "I had something else in mind, but if you're into that kind of thing, I'm happy to oblige."

She didn't always hear his unique accent—or at least she found it to be one of a kind. She'd spent plenty of time in and around Massachusetts, and while he didn't have a strong Bostonian accent, traces of it came out when he said certain words or phrases. Other times he sounded more like someone who'd spent their life in New York City. She'd never spent a lot of time in New Hampshire, where he'd grown up, so she wasn't sure if his accent was unique to him or shared by everyone from that area. Either way, this afternoon it was making a subtle appearance.

"I'd rather see what you already had planned." She'd also like to know why he was holding a pot that contained minia-ture pink roses, but first things first.

Ryan didn't keep her waiting. After setting the plant down, he moved forward and cupped the back of her head before claiming her lips. Slowly, his mouth moved over hers, each pass hungrier than the one before it.

As if they had a mind of their own, her lips parted. When Ryan's tongue touched hers, ecstasy like she'd never experienced spiraled through her body, and assuming her knees didn't turn to complete mush and give out, she'd happily spend the rest of the afternoon doing exactly this.

A gentle nudge to the back of her thigh cut through the sensual fog clouding her brain. Reluctantly, she pulled back, because once Marley started demanding attention, he rarely gave up until he got it.

"Much better than a scratch behind the ears." She lowered her hand that had somehow found its way to Ryan's shoulder.

"Good. That's what I was aiming for." Ryan's accent was a smidge more pronounced now, and there was no mistaking the rapid pulse in his neck, a clear indicator their kiss affected him too. Then, perhaps just remembering the plant he'd carried in, he picked it up. "Happy birthday."

She eyed the miniature roses before finally accepting them.

"I know most people bring bouquets, not plants. But cut flowers never last long. It's why my mom always told my father not to waste his money. I figured this way you could plant these in the yard." He withdrew an envelope from his back pocket and held it toward her. "But this is your actual birthday present."

Had he run some kind of background check on her? He worked for a private security firm. Perhaps they could do such things. Then again, a search on the internet might turn up the results. Either way, she didn't like the idea of him looking for information about her. Especially since if he wanted to know something about her, all he had to do was ask. It wasn't like she had any secrets to hide.

"The roses are beautiful, and you're right, arrangements

from the florist never last long. But how did you know today is my birthday? I'm pretty sure I never told you." Actually, she was positive she'd never told him.

"The calendar hanging up in your kitchen. When I was over last week, I noticed your birthday marked on it."

Ah, yes, the photo calendar hanging up on her kitchen wall. Every year her goddaughter made her a calendar for Christmas. In addition to the monthly holidays, Shelly always made sure both her and Kenzie's birthdays were clearly marked. On this year's calendar, she'd not only added Kenzie's name to today's square, but she'd added a picture of a birthday cake too.

"Good eyes. But you didn't need to get me anything." With her question answered, she accepted the plain white envelope. Nothing about it provided any clue as to what was inside.

"I wanted to."

Slipping her fingernail under the tape, Kenzie opened the envelope and pulled out the contents. "Tickets to see the Nationals." She hadn't been to a game in a long time. Neither of the previous two men she'd dated had been interested in baseball, and the thought of going alone made it less appealing.

"Unfortunately, they not playing at home this weekend, so I had to get them for next Saturday. I hope you don't already have plans."

Okay, he learned today was her birthday thanks to the calendar, but how did he know she'd enjoy seeing the Nationals play? The topic of sports hadn't come up in any of their conversations. Tickets to a major league baseball game weren't cheap. Most people wouldn't want to dish out the money if they didn't already know the individual receiving them was a fan.

Kenzie put the tickets away and kissed his cheek. "I do

now. And since there are two, it looks like you do too. I've got to ask. How did you know I'm a Nationals fan?"

If she had a team flag flying in front of the house or a bumper sticker on her car, she'd understand how he'd figured it out. But the only flag flying outside the house was the American flag, and there wasn't a single bumper sticker on her car.

"When you work outside, you usually wear a Nationals baseball hat. And I've seen you wearing one of their sweatshirts."

Okay, he'd really impressed her. Not only did Ryan notice things most people would overlook, he used the information to get her something she'd love. "Observant, aren't you?"

"You could say it's a requirement for my job."

"I'm almost afraid to ask what other details you've learned about me." She nodded toward Marley, who was still sitting near her feet. "I only need to feed Marley, and then I'm ready to go." At the word feed, Marley trotted off to the kitchen, leaving Kenzie and Ryan to follow.

"Take your time. There's no rush."

Kenzie left the roses and the tickets on the kitchen counter. If he wasn't in a rush, that suggested their destination didn't require tickets or reservations. And Ryan was dressed as casually as she was in cargo shorts and a T-shirt.

She could feel his gaze on her as she walked toward the closet where she kept the dog food. "Are you going to tell me now what we're up to, or do I need to wait?"

He seemed to consider her question before answering. "We're going to Meadow Valley."

Kenzie tried to place the name. It sounded vaguely familiar. "Isn't that a golf course?" Other than to play mini-golf, she'd never picked up a golf club in her life, but with possibly the exception of skydiving, she'd try anything at least once.

"Meadow Hill is a country club and golf course. Meadow

Valley is a botanical garden. You spend so much time gardening, it seemed like a place you would enjoy."

She'd never seen Ryan do anything in his yard but mow the lawn and rake the leaves. A botanical garden sounded like the last place he'd want to hang out for the afternoon. The fact he was taking her there because he guessed how much she loved flowers and gardening impressed her. All right, it did more than impress her. It put yet another check mark in the "I really like this man" category. Not that it needed many more.

"If it's anything like the one in D.C., I'll love it." She preferred not to drive in D.C., so she didn't go often. When she headed to the capital, the United States Botanical Garden was often among the places she visited, but it had been a long time since her last visit.

He'd planned for everything today except the suspicious look Kenzie gave him when he wished her a happy birthday. In hindsight, he should've expected it. Thanks to the internet, it was fairly easy for anyone to learn everything from when a person was born to what schools they'd attended. The resources he had access to at work made it even easier. Even those with nothing to hide didn't like others searching through their backgrounds, and he didn't blame them.

He held her hand as they crossed the lawn separating their yards, and although it was a stupid thought, he couldn't get past the fact it felt perfect there.

"New car?"

He'd backed his pride and joy into his driveway before walking over to Kenzie's house. Unless it was a picture-perfect day, the 1965 Shelby Mustang he'd restored didn't leave his garage. Today's weather promised to be such a day.

Ryan didn't open car doors for his dates, and the women

he usually went out with didn't expect him to. But like Spike said this morning, he was doing things differently with Kenzie.

"No. I just haven't had many opportunities to use it this summer."

While everyone knew Elite Force provided private security to anyone who could afford it, the forty-plus-year-old firm did a hell of a lot more, especially the Hostile Response Team. Earlier in the summer, the firm had tasked HRT with the job of rescuing a mom and her young daughter who were being held in Mexico against their will. He and Spike led the mission and spent almost three weeks south of the border. Not long after his return, he'd taken a short vacation to visit his family before being tapped to escort a big-mouthed oil guy from Texas down to South America. Although the guy regularly used the firm to protect him when he traveled outside the country, this was the first time Ryan had worked for the ass. The next time the guy hired the firm, and he would, he hoped someone else drew the short straw. One experience with Stan Bonds was enough.

"And it never leaves the garage in the winter." He waited for Kenzie to get comfortable before closing the door and walking around the front of the convertible.

"Any chance I can drive later?" She gave him a damn good version of puppy dog eyes. The very expression that always had him caving when either his niece or nephew turned it on him.

Releasing the clutch, he pressed down the accelerator and backed into the street. "Depends, how good are you at driving a standard?" He'd spent too many hours on the car to let just anyone behind the wheel, no matter how much he liked her, and risk burning out the clutch or worse.

Kenzie patted the dashboard. "Don't worry, I'll take good care of your baby. My first two cars were standards."

When it came to plants and flowers, his knowledge was very limited, and he had no desire to expand upon it. So if he were looking for a way to pass some time, visiting a botanical garden wouldn't be on his radar. Today wasn't about him and what he enjoyed. Nope, today he wanted to make Kenzie's birthday special and see her smile. A few hours walking around this place should accomplish his goal.

Vehicles filled the parking lot, and it took him a few passes up and down the aisles before he found them a spot. According to the website, the garden encompassed ninety-five acres of displays and walking trails. Hopefully, with that much real estate available to explore, the place wouldn't feel as busy as it looked.

He intended to open the door for her like he had earlier, but by the time he got to her side, Kenzie was out of the car and waiting for him.

"Have you ever been here?" she asked.

"You've seen my yard. The closest I've ever gotten to a place like this was the gardening section at the hardware store the last time I needed a rake."

With a small laugh, Kenzie reached down and threaded her fingers through his. "I guessed as much. But how did you know about this place?"

"A friend of mine at work loves flowers like you. When I asked for some suggestions, Alex recommended this."

One of only two women on the Hostile Response Team, Alexandra Thompson was a walking contradiction. On so many levels she was the stereotypical girly-girl. She loved fashion, much like his younger sister, enjoyed keeping up with celebrity news, and even drove a pink car. At the same time, Alex shot as well as, if not better than, the rest of the guys on the team, and when it came to hand-to-hand combat, she could hold her own.

Kenzie preceded him into the visitor center, a large brick building with flowers and shrubs all around it. "Was he at your cookout?"

"No. She couldn't make it. But I think the two of you would get along well. Her yard is almost as impressive as yours."

Visitors filled the gift shop off to the left, but otherwise, the building was fairly empty considering the number of cars out front. Mounted on the wall was a display of brochures in various languages. "Should we grab one or just wander and see where we end up?" Kenzie asked.

He couldn't think of anything worse than not having a plan. "Let's get one. There might be an area you really want to check out."

The inside of the informational brochure contained a detailed map and a corresponding key. It also gave a brief history of the garden and listed ways individuals could support the facility both financially as well as through volunteer work.

"Anything jumping out at you?" The place contained everything from a Korean Bell Garden and hosta collection to a children's tearoom.

Accepting the map, Kenzie studied it closer. "How about we head up this way?" She traced the walking trail that exited out the rear of the visitor center and continued past the seasonal plantings toward the spot labeled Great Lawn. "It looks like there is a lot to see here, and we can check out the Korean Bell Garden." She pointed toward the large white space before tracing another black line away from it. "Then maybe we can take this trail over to the lilac pavilion and the hosta collection."

His grandparents had a lilac bush in their backyard, so he

knew what they were. Ryan had no damn idea what a hosta was, but it looked like he was about to find out.

She pointed to one of the many gazebo-style structures dotting the map. "We should've brought food with us. It looks like there are a lot of good places to have a picnic."

He'd considered it when Alex mentioned there were several great spots designed for that purpose. However, at least for tonight, he preferred the idea of a private dinner alone. "I thought about it. But I have a special meal planned for you when we get back. If you want, we can come back here some other time and bring a picnic." Unless she flat-out told him to get lost, he planned on spending more time with her after today.

They spent a fair amount of time exploring the Great Lawn, and Kenzie made sure to point out and label the various plants and trees growing in the area, most of which he'd never remember the names of. A large koi pond sat in the center, and they stopped long enough to see the various colorful fish swimming around. Unless they were on his dinner plate, he'd never had much interest in fish. The ones swimming around were unique, and he could understand why some people would want similar structures in their yards or fish tanks in their homes.

After a quick stop at the gazebo located in the center of the man-made lake, they headed toward the pagoda containing the enormous bell constructed in South Korea. Situated on the top of a hill, the area was filled with replicas of ancient Korean statues and stone walls adorned with traditional Korean symbols. It was unlike any other part of the garden they'd seen so far. Considering all the people around taking pictures, this area was a popular photo spot. And it wasn't only garden visitors snapping away. There was also a professional photographer trying to arrange a wedding party while at the same time keeping other people from getting in the way.

They stopped several feet away, so they wouldn't bother the wedding party or the photographer. "It's a great backdrop for pictures, but I would've picked an area with more color," Kenzie commented.

In his opinion, a picture was all about the people in it. Whether there were flowers in the background or a giant bell didn't matter.

"Where to next?" This was her day, so he was following her lead.

Kenzie pointed toward a trail on the map. "Let's head this way."

The path took them down the other side of the hill and around the children's garden and tearoom. This afternoon the area was swarming with kids, some who could barely walk, while others looked to be twelve or thirteen. Despite the word garden in its description, the area was basically a playground, with a large swing set complete with slides, monkey bars, and areas for the children to dig. Near the entrance was a decent-sized building. Large windows allowed him to see inside. While one room contained several long tables and chairs, the other one looked full of more hands-on activities.

Once past the children's area, the trail changed from a paved one to dirt as it wound its way through a tree grove.

"I think the lilacs will be the last thing we see today," she said, clearly disappointed.

A glance at his watch confirmed her theory. Meadow Valley closed in an hour. If the amount of time she'd spent in the Great Lawn was any indication, they'd be looking at lilacs for a while, not to mention they still needed to make it back to the visitor center before they locked the doors for the night.

"According to the website, this place is open year-round. They have something called the Winter Walk of Light starting later in the year. So we've got plenty of time to come back and check out whatever we miss today."

Up ahead, an area filled with various hues of purple and white signaled they were just about at their final destination. But Kenzie stopped and turned to face him. With no hesitation, she circled her arms over his shoulders and skimmed her lips across his.

"I plan to hold you to that, Mr. Saltarelli."

FOUR

At least in terms of layout, Ryan's house was identical to hers. The entire first floor was open, with the dining room, living room, and kitchen all flowing into each other. One door in the kitchen opened into the fenced-in backyard, while another one went into the attached garage. A staircase hugged the wall in the living room, leading to the upstairs, and a second one extended into the finished basement where a large laundry room was located. Although in her house it also doubled as Marley's bedroom when she was out. Actually, all the homes in their community were similar both on the inside and the outside. Each had the same basic floor plan, with the only true difference being the final dimensions and the number of bedrooms. However, to keep things uniform, the developers organized the house sizes by street. So while all the homes on their street contained two bedrooms, the ones two streets over were larger.

"You know your way around the kitchen." From her spot at the kitchen island, Kenzie watched him retrieve more ingredients from the refrigerator. She'd been sitting there for at least the past ten minutes watching him work and enjoying the show. Of course, she'd enjoy watching Ryan clean toilets if it meant she could look at him.

Ryan placed two sage leaves on top of a chicken cutlet and then wrapped a slice of prosciutto around it. "My first job was working at my grandparents' restaurant. I was there every weekend during the school year and all summer long. When I was in college, I'd work there during breaks."

"What did you do there?" She'd tried waitressing once, her freshman year of college. Since she loved to cook, a restaurant had seemed like a good place to get a part-time job. She lasted three months before quitting and getting a job at the mall instead. Although she hadn't loved working retail either, she stuck with it until she graduated. No matter how hard she tried, Kenzie couldn't picture Ryan waiting tables or working in the kitchen. Although, if he had waited tables, he'd probably caught the attention of a lot of the restaurant's patrons.

"A little of everything. We all did." He wrapped the next cutlet on the plate. "I started busing tables and moved on to waiting tables. Later, I worked as a line cook."

She snagged a slice of prosciutto before he could stop her, and he pulled the meat closer to his side of the counter. "Do your grandparents still own the restaurant?" They hadn't gone into great detail about their families, and she wanted to know more about him.

"No. Five or six years ago, they sold the place to my mom and aunt so they could be snowbirds. Aunt Tracey sold her half to my sister, Vanessa, a few years ago when her grandson was born. She takes care of him while my cousin and her husband are at work. At some point, Vanessa will take over the whole place." He finished wrapping the last chicken cutlet and gestured toward the remaining prosciutto. "Help yourself."

"Just one more slice." Back in the spring, they'd both

been outside working in their yards when Ryan mentioned his sister was coming for a visit, but she had never met her. "Is she the one who stayed with you in April?"

Ryan shook his head as he washed his hands. "My younger sister, Melinda, came down. I don't think Vanessa has ever visited me here. Since she became part owner, she doesn't travel much further than Boston."

Growing up an only child, she'd often wished for a sibling, preferably a sister, but she would've been happy with either. "Is it just the three of you?"

"No. I also have three brothers."

She couldn't imagine growing up in a house with so many people. "Six kids? Your poor mom and dad."

After adding olive oil to a large skillet, he turned on the stove and returned to the counter for the wrapped cutlets. "Mom always made it look easy, but yeah, sometimes I wonder how she and my dad survived."

"Melinda is younger than you, but what about the rest?"

"Kyle's the oldest, and Vanessa is a year younger than him. Ben's the baby of the family. Melinda is almost two years younger than my twin Adam and me. What about you? Any brothers or sisters?"

"Nope. But my cousin Megan is like a sister. I keep trying to get her to move here, but so far I've had no luck." She understood her cousin's reasons for not wanting to leave New York, but it didn't stop her from suggesting it every so often. "With six kids, your house must have never been a dull place."

"Or quiet. And forget about taking a long time in the bathroom. My parents had their own, but the six of us shared the other two."

Senior year in college, she'd rented an apartment with two friends rather than live on campus. Although they'd each had a separate bedroom, they shared the single bathroom. It had taken them several weeks to work out a morning schedule so everyone could shower and make it to class on time. She couldn't imagine having to share with five other people.

"Do all your brothers and sisters still live in New Hampshire?" Kenzie watched as he started on another part of the dish. She didn't know what he was making, but it looked good.

"Everyone except Adam. He's down in North Carolina, at least for now. He put his name in for a Legat position in England."

"Your brother's an FBI agent?" Legat wasn't a word dropped every day, and unless a person was familiar with federal government lingo, most wouldn't know what it meant —which explained Ryan's expression. "Around the same time that my dad transferred to the field office in Norfolk, a good friend of his went to work as a legal attaché in Germany."

The confusion disappeared from Ryan's face. "Adam graduated from the academy about five months after I did. Your dad is an agent?"

"Was. He retired about three and a half years ago. Now Dad and Reggie, the one who worked as a Legat, own a self-defense and firearms school in Woodbridge together."

He poured two glasses of white wine and handed her one before adding some to the saucepan on the stove.

"Mom worked for the Bureau too, as a forensic photographer. They met when they were both working in the Houston field office. A couple of years after I was born, they transferred to Albany, New York."

"Does your mom still work for the Bureau?" Ryan added chicken broth to the pan and glanced over at her as he stirred the sauce he was preparing.

Sipping her wine, Kenzie shook her head. "She retired

about a year before my dad. Now she spends her time photographing weddings and doing family portraits. I think she enjoys it a lot more too."

She started to reach for another slice of prosciutto but then pulled her hand back. Ryan was going to a lot of effort to make her dinner. She didn't want to be already full and unable to enjoy whatever he was making when it was ready. "Why did you leave the FBI?"

The moment he mentioned he'd graduated the FBI Academy in Quantico, he'd expected that question. Almost everyone who learned about his previous career asked it or something very similar. And he understood why. The FBI was selective. Most of the people who applied each year didn't even make it to the interview phase of the application process. Of those who did and made it to the academy, some washed out before graduating. Considering all the time and hard work a person put in to earn the title special agent, most individuals didn't quit six years into their career.

"The easy answer is because I got tired of the BS. I worked with some great people and handled some good cases, but too often politics and red tape prevents agents from doing what they need to. It didn't help that the assistant special agent in charge of the San Juan office was an ass. He didn't care about getting stuff done. His only concern was furthering his career."

Removing the chicken from the skillet, he put two cutlets on each plate before spooning sauce over them. Then he carried the plates to the table and returned for the spinach salad and fettuccini alfredo.

"Dad has complained about a few ASACs he's worked for too. According to him, the one who started at the Albany office a few months before he and Mom transferred to

Norfolk was by far the worst. But he's had some great ones too." She turned on her barstool to face him. "Can I help with anything?"

Using the salad bowl, he pointed toward the wine on the counter. "Can you bring over our glasses and the bottle of wine?"

Grabbing both, she hopped off the barstool and followed him to the kitchen table.

Earlier in the day, he'd toyed with the idea of getting candles for the table. In the end, he'd dismissed it. Now he wished he'd grabbed some. He found eating by candlelight annoying, but a lot of women considered it romantic. Since he couldn't do anything about the lighting situation, he set down the food and pulled her chair out before she could do it. It was something he couldn't remember ever doing for a woman, but he'd seen his dad and his grandfather do it occasionally. And guys in old black-and-white movies always did it when they were trying to be a gentlemen.

"How many field offices did your parents work out of?" Some agents spent their whole careers in the same office, while others moved around every few years. He'd spent the first two years of his career in Phoenix before being transferred to the office in Puerto Rico. His brother started his career in New Orleans, perhaps the most unique city Ryan had ever visited, before going to North Carolina.

"Only three. They both began their careers in the Houston office, and then they requested to be sent to the one in Albany because Dad's family is in the area. It's not too far from my mom's parents either. They live in the western part of Massachusetts. After I graduated college and they realized I wasn't moving back to New York, they asked for a transfer down here. They wanted something closer to me, but Norfolk was the only office with openings."

"When Adam and I first moved out of state, Mom used

to ask us to find a way to get transferred back to New England. I think she's finally accepted that it might never happen."

If the restaurant was his mom's life, then her family was her heart and soul. To her, nothing was more important than her children and grandchildren. If the woman could somehow clone herself so she could be in New Hampshire, Virginia, and North Carolina all at the same time, she would in a heartbeat.

While he waited for Kenzie to take what she wanted of the salad, he refilled their wineglasses. When she finished, she passed him the bowl.

"Ryan, this looks and smells amazing. What is it?"

"Saltimbocca. Traditionally, it's made with veal. A lot of people don't eat veal, including me, so my grandmother started making it with chicken as well at the restaurant. I hope you like it."

After Kenzie added fettuccini to her plate, she reached for her utensils. "I'm glad you went with the chicken instead. I'm not a fan of veal either." She cut a corner off the cutlet and popped it in her mouth.

Following her lead, he dug into his meal. He'd never gotten around to eating lunch, and he was starving.

She took another bite of the chicken before sampling the pasta and salad. "Wow, this is delicious. I think you missed your calling."

He'd worked enough in a restaurant to know it wasn't for him. "I enjoy cooking but could never spend my life working in a kitchen. I'll leave that to my sister."

With food in her mouth, Kenzie nodded and swallowed. "I know what you mean. I tried working at a restaurant in college. It wasn't for me. But I do love experimenting with dishes." She took a sip of her wine before she continued. "So, if you were with the FBI in San Juan, how did you end up working for Elite Force? Do private security firms put ads in the help wanted section or something?"

"Spike gave my name to the director. He knew I was unhappy working for the government and thought I would be a good fit."

"I remember him from the cookout. Was he an agent too before working for Elite Force?"

"No. Spike and I grew up together. He spent more time at my house than his own. Spike only has sisters. He even calls my parents Mom and Dad."

"What about you, are you close to Spike's family?"

Ryan cut into his chicken and then scooped up some noodles. "Yeah. They're down here for the next few days. Spike's younger sister is looking at colleges. I'm hoping to get over and see them before they go home."

"I've got to ask. Is Spike his actual name?"

Other than Ryan, no one at work knew how his friend got his nickname. No one asked either. They just accepted it.

"No. His name is Jonathan, like his dad. When we were in first grade, he got his hands on some extra-strong glue. I don't know what kind it was. He used to see his mom put gel and stuff in her hair and decided to do it with the glue and spiked it like a character from a cartoon we used to watch. For the next week or so, he came to school with his hair spiked in crazy directions because shampoo wouldn't take the glue out. Kids started calling him Spike, and it stuck."

"How long did it take his mom to get the glue out?"

"I don't remember, but she was pissed when she found out what he'd used."

"And let me guess, you stood there and watched while he did it?"

He couldn't stop himself from smiling as the full memory surfaced. "Nah, I was the lookout. I stayed in the hall outside the bathroom door in case his mom or older sister came down the hall. They never did."

———

Ryan placed the small birthday cake he purchased at the bakery on the patio table. "Sorry, I forgot to pick up candles."

Kenzie crossed her arms. "That's completely unacceptable. I'm not sure I want to be friends with you anymore."

She was trying to sound serious, but he saw the smiling tugging at her lips.

"What if I make it up to you?" Ryan sat next to her and put his arm over her shoulders.

Kenzie considered his words for a moment before shaking her head. "I don't think it's possible. A birthday cake needs candles. Without them, it's just another cake with frosting."

Leaning closer, he stopped before his lips landed on hers. "I still want to try." Ryan traced the soft fullness of her lips and then skimmed his mouth across hers. It took some effort, but he managed not to linger there. "Are we still friends?" Regardless of her answer, he had no intention of stopping at the moment.

"Forgetting birthday candles is a big deal, Ryan. Everyone knows that."

Ryan captured her lips just as she was finishing her sentence. Moving his mouth over hers, he devoured its softness. And when she parted her lips, inviting him inside, he didn't hesitate. A shot of desire raced through him when their tongues touched. Reaching behind her, he removed the hair tie holding her ponytail in place and ran his fingers through her hair like he'd wanted to do this morning. As he did, he pictured Kenzie naked in his bed with her hair spread across his pillow as they made love. His body reacted to the image, and he struggled to hold back a groan.

Changing the angle of his lips, he deepened the kiss as Kenzie's hands went from his shoulders to the base of his head. Her fingernails raked through his hair, adding to the hunger already prowling through his body and urging him to invite her upstairs for the night.

Kenzie's different. A small voice pushed its way through the fog clouding his head. Ending their kiss was the last thing he wanted, but if he didn't do it now, he wouldn't be able to. Ryan allowed himself one last brush across her lips before pulling away and hoped she didn't look any lower than his chest, because she'd never miss the erection straining against his shorts.

When she met his gaze and he saw the same fire raging inside him reflected in her eyes, the desire to strip her naked and lay her down on the ground only intensified. "Still friends?" As if it had a mind of its own, his hand lingered in her hair, loving the way the soft strands cascaded over his skin.

Slowly, she traced her index finger along his jaw and then continued down his neck before settling on the rapid pulse in his neck. "For now. But if you do that every time one of your friends is upset with you, we will have a problem."

"I'll remember that." If he kissed her mouth again, it'd be all over, so instead he took her hand and pressed his lips against her palm.

Despite the lack of candles, Ryan offered to sing "Happy Birthday." Much to his relief, she insisted it wasn't necessary, because him singing wouldn't be a pleasant experience for anyone present. And today had been all about making Kenzie's birthday special.

After cutting two large slices of cake, he switched on the large outdoor television mounted to the house.

"It's not the same as being there, but I thought we could watch the ball game out here. If you want to do something else, just say the word." He knew what he'd rather be doing, but he didn't think it was an option tonight.

"Depends. If I wasn't here, would you be watching the game?"

Digging his fork into the cake, Ryan shook his head. "Nah. I only watch Boston's games, when I can get them."

"Then let's skip it."

"Are you sure?"

"Positive. We're going to the game next weekend." She licked the frosting off her finger before taking another forkful of cake.

The baseball game would have kept her there for a few more hours. With it off the table, there was nothing to keep her around once she finished the cake, and it might make him a selfish SOB, but he wasn't ready to call it a night. "Interested in a movie?"

"Sure. What do you have?"

More like what didn't he have. He'd always been a movie buff and had everything from classic black-and-white films to the latest box office hits. "A little of everything. Name a genre and I'll tell you what I have."

"Musicals."

He couldn't tell if she was serious or not. "Sorry. No musicals."

"They're not my thing either. I was just curious." She took another forkful of cake. "How about something with a little suspense?"

That he could do. "Do you want something recent or an older movie?"

Kenzie considered his question before answering. "Older. Maybe a Hitchcock movie if you have one."

"I have most of his movies. Which one do you want to see?" His mom was a Hitchcock fan, and she'd introduced him to the man's movies.

"Do you have *North by Northwest*?"

It wasn't his favorite, but he enjoyed it. Picking up the remote, he logged into his movie collection and hit Play.

Next to him, she took a final forkful of cake before setting the rest aside. "If you have most of his movies, you must be a Hitchcock fan. What's your favorite?"

"I'd have to go with *Rear Window*." More than half his cake remained, but with her so close, he wouldn't pass on an opportunity to touch her. After putting his plate on a table, Ryan slipped his arm over her shoulders. And as if they'd sat like this a hundred times, she immediately leaned against him.

"Probably my third favorite. *North by Northwest* is at the top of my list, followed by *Vertigo*." Kenzie rested her head on his shoulder, where it seemed to fit perfectly in the hollow between his shoulder and neck.

On the screen, the opening scene played out. "Any plans for tomorrow after work?"

"My parents are coming up for my birthday and staying the night."

Looked like he might visit with Spike and his family tomorrow after all.

"They're taking me to Fleming's Grill for dinner. Come with us."

He hadn't met a woman's parents since his senior year of college. Most of the women he'd dated since then hadn't been looking for anything but some fun and sex. Until recently he'd been content with that. Not anymore. Since his sister gave birth to her second child back in February, he'd started to notice all the things both she and their older brother had and he didn't. The minivan he'd pass on, but a partner to share his life with, he'd take.

"Are you sure they won't mind?" Judging by what she'd told him, she had a close relationship with her parents. They might not like some random dude suddenly showing up for a special dinner with their baby girl.

"Positive. My parents should be here around five." Lifting her head, she kissed his cheek. "I'll need some time to get ready after work, but I should be done by about four. Come on over anytime after then."

Looked like tomorrow he was meeting Mr. and Mrs. Armstrong. "Will do." With her lips so close to his, he couldn't resist kissing her.

FIVE

Before leaving for work, Kenzie let her parents know she'd invited someone special to join them tonight for dinner. And no question about it, Ryan was special. Long after she'd left his house last night and climbed into bed, she reflected on the effort he'd put in to make the day special. Other than her parents, she couldn't remember anyone ever working so hard to make sure she enjoyed her birthday, and she had some incredibly thoughtful friends and relatives.

Thanks to Ryan's actions and knee-melting kisses, Kenzie assumed they'd crossed from the "let's see if we like each other" stage to the "no longer dating other people" stage. The fact he'd agreed to dinner with her parents tonight supported her assumption. Generally, she hated to assume anything. At the same time, asking Ryan if she was his girlfriend struck her as something thirteen-year-old girls did, so at least for the time being, she'd assume and hope she didn't make an ass of herself in the end.

With a towel wrapped around her body, Kenzie checked her wristwatch on the nightstand before opening the closet door and revealing her somewhat limited wardrobe. Her idea of getting dressed up involved a pair of jeans and a nice top rather than a T-shirt. Unfortunately, jeans were out tonight. Although the Fleming Grill didn't require evening gowns and tuxedos, you didn't walk inside looking like you just came from a shopping trip to the mall.

Kenzie pushed aside the heavy sweaters hanging up, along with her ski jacket and favorite Washington Nationals sweatshirt. She'd never been big into wearing dresses and skirts. Even as a child when she played dress-up, she'd skipped the princess gowns and opted for either the doctor scrubs or the firefighter jacket, and forget about wearing tights. The only year she'd taken dance, she'd been forced to wear tights to every class and to the recital. After that year, she'd tossed out all her tights, dived into team sports, and never looked back. Her view on the offending piece of clothing hadn't changed since then either. She didn't even own a pair of pantyhose, and nowadays the tightest article of clothing she wore were the occasional leggings.

Sundresses were the one exception. Since she could keep her legs bare under them, she owned several and wore them often in the summer. While some of the ones in her closet were far too casual for dinner tonight, a few would do. Kenzie pulled out the floral lilac one she'd purchased back in June when she took her goddaughter shopping. After cutting the tags off, she tossed it on the bed and went in search of underwear. When it came to clothes, she opted for ones that were comfortable and practical. Her choice in underwear followed the same logic. She'd tried thongs and found nothing comfortable about a piece of fabric stuck between her butt cheeks all day long. Give her a pair of cotton bikini briefs and she was happy. The same was true of her bras. She didn't want some padded contraption pushing her boobs up to her chin. Regardless of her preference for everyday wear, she owned a handful of lacy thongs and hip huggers and their matching bras. She only wore them when she expected someone besides her to see them. Last night she'd considered putting on a matching set, but in the end, opted to stick with her usual. It turned out to be the right move, because Ryan never attempted to get her out of her shorts and T-shirt—a fact that raised a whole host of emotions, including disappointment and surprise.

She didn't make a habit of sleeping with every man she went on a date with. However, if Ryan had taken things between them further last night like she suspected he wanted to, she wouldn't have stopped him even though they hadn't been dating long. And there wasn't a doubt in her mind he'd wanted to have sex last night. She'd tried not to stare, but there had been no missing the erection he suffered with through much of the movie. Later, when he walked her home and pulled her against him, she'd felt it pressing into her lower belly. In fact, she'd almost invited him in so they could satisfy the desire they were both dealing with, because he hadn't been the only one. She was turned on almost to the breaking point by the time they arrived at her front door. Sure, they'd turned on a movie, but they hadn't simply sat there and watched it from beginning to end. Instead, they'd taken breaks from what was on the screen to engage in more pleasurable and heart-racing ways of passing the time.

Closing her eyes, Kenzie could almost feel his fingers teasing her nipple again as he demonstrated what a master he was when it came to kissing. She'd had her first boyfriend at sixteen, so she'd kissed her fair share of guys. None had ever kissed her in such a way that her entire body responded. Somehow Ryan had managed it.

Although only a delightful memory, her nipples responded, straining against the bath towel, begging for Ryan's touch. Yup, if he'd stripped her bare last night, she wouldn't have stopped him. When he finished, she would've returned the favor and helped him out of his shorts and T-shirt.

In her head, the memory of him touching her breasts ended and her imagination took over. Rather than keeping the evening PG-rated, Ryan tugged both their clothes off before pleasuring her with his mouth and tongue, his barely-there beard brushing against the sensitive skin on her inner thighs as he did. Then while she still rode the high of her orgasm, he joined their bodies and took her over the top again. Taking in a slow breath, she allowed her imagination to keep going. It didn't disappoint. Now, instead of Ryan pleasuring her, she set about seeing to his needs.

The sound of a sleigh bell intruded on the X-rated daydream, and Kenzie opened her eyes. The whole thing might have happened in her head, but her body ached for Ryan's hands and mouth. She might daydream from time to time, but they were never erotic. Considering the way she felt at the moment, it was a good thing her imagination usually stayed kid friendly.

When she picked up her cell phone, a picture of a cartoon butt dancing greeted her. She didn't need to check the number to know who the text message was from. Only Megan would send her a dancing butt instead of a hello. A message from her cousin appeared on the screen before Kenzie typed any kind of reply.

Do you have time to talk? I want to know how your date was last night.

They never managed to keep a conversation less than thirty minutes, and she didn't have that kind of time right now. Ryan, as well as her parents, would be there soon, and thanks to her X-rated daydream, she wasn't even dressed.

Not really, my parents will be here soon. I'll call you tomorrow.

A pair of pouting lips appeared on the screen followed by another message.

Okay, but at least tell me if you had a good time.

"Good" didn't adequately describe the day. Even "great" wasn't quite right, but for now, it would have to suffice because a better one didn't come to mind.

I had a great time. Tell you about it later.

I'm glad. Look forward to hearing about it. Say hi to your parents for me.

Will do.

Setting the device down, she went back to getting ready before she again got distracted by her vivid imagination. A mix of various colors stared back up at her from the drawer. For a moment, her hand hovered over the pale pink lacy thong. Then she pushed it aside and grabbed a pair of cotton panties instead. Even if Ryan came back to her house after dinner, her parents were spending the night. She might be an adult and this might be her house, but she still didn't want her parents sleeping down the hall while she and Ryan had sex for the first time. Something told her Ryan would have a similar view. Going back to his house instead would solve that problem, but ditching her parents who had driven up for her birthday so she could get laid was out of the question.

After fastening a necklace around her neck, Kenzie moved in front of the mirror. A sight she wasn't all too familiar with greeted her. Unlike most days, her hair wasn't pulled back in a ponytail or bun so it wouldn't fall in her face all day and drive her crazy. Instead, thanks to a hairdryer—which it had taken ten minutes to find because it had been so long since she last used it—and a styling brush, it hung around her shoulders in gentle waves. While she wore a touch of makeup to work every day, she never bothered with anything around her eyes, and forget about lipstick. On the rare occasion she wore the stuff, it was all over the rim of her travel coffee mug by the time she got to the clinic, so she saw no reason to bother with it. Today she'd gone all out though, and thanks to her cousin's lessons she didn't look like a three-year-old who'd gotten into her mother's makeup bag.

Turning away from the mirror, she looked at Marley. At the moment, he was playing with a miniature rubber tire on the floor, oblivious to anything else. "What do you think, Marley?" At the sound of his name, he looked up, cocked his head and one ear, then went back to what he'd been doing.

"I will take that as a compliment."

From the other side of the door, Ryan heard Marley barking, letting Kenzie and their neighbors know someone had rung her doorbell. Raking a hand through his hair, he glanced around for any approaching cars. Although he'd intended to skip the gym and mow his grass before going over to Kenzie's at four, well before her parents arrived, it hadn't happened. Instead, he'd agreed to meet Keith at the gym for a few rounds on the mats, a decision he was regretting now. Not only did a traffic backup cause him to get home later than he'd planned, but thanks to Keith's elbow he had a fabulous black eye. Meeting your girlfriend's parents, or whatever label she wanted him to use, with a black eye was not the best way to make a good first impression. If the bruise wasn't bad enough, he still had a heavy metal drummer going at it in his head thanks to his sparring session with Keith, despite the ibuprofen he'd taken before he jumped in the shower. Perhaps the only consolation to the events of the day so far was that Keith hadn't walked away unscathed either.

When Kenzie opened the door, she didn't greet him with a kiss like he'd hoped she would or even a hello. "Yikes. What happened to you?" She touched his cheek just below the bruise and searched his face for any other injuries while

Marley came forward and nudged his leg, looking for some attention.

"I sparred with Keith today, and I didn't get my face out of the way fast enough." Perhaps if his head had been on the mats instead of on Kenzie and how perfectly her breast had fit in his hand last night, he would have avoided his buddy's elbow. Then again, maybe not—when it came to ground fighting, Keith was one of the best in the group.

Taking his hand, she drew him inside and closed the door. "Is that the only place he got you?"

"If I say no, will you feel obligated to give me a complete physical and take care of my injuries?" Yesterday Keith had teased him about playing doctor with Kenzie, and he couldn't think of a more pleasurable way to spend the rest of the evening.

Releasing his hand, she smiled, and it was like Keith had sucker-punched him in the gut. Explaining the effect Kenzie's smile had on him was beyond his capabilities, so Ryan didn't even bother to analyze it. Instead, he planted a kiss on her parted lips. Pulling her in closer, he slipped his hands over her bare shoulders and down the portion of her back left exposed by her sundress. Beneath his hands, fabric replaced her smooth skin, and he continued south until his palms settled on her exquisite ass. Much like her breasts and smile, visions of her ass had kept him hard long past the time she left last night.

Kenzie groaned when he gave her ass a little squeeze; then she pulled her mouth away. "I would, but we don't have time."

Reaching between them, she ran her fingers down his chest and stomach. She'd done something similar last night, and he'd thought she intended to unfasten the button of his shorts. Unfortunately, she'd only let her fingers linger near his waistband before reversing the trip and settling on his shoulder. This time, her fingers didn't linger. They slipped past his belt buckle, and her palm settled over his zipper.

Rubbing her hand against him, she held his gaze. "But I wish we did."

If he didn't stop her, he would embarrass himself or worse, because in another minute or two he was going to push her dress up around her waist and make love to her against the wall. But damn, her hand felt good against him, and removing it went against every cell in his body. While he still had the willpower, he grabbed her wrist and pulled her hand away. If he had any hope of behaving himself between now and when her parents arrived, he needed to start a conversation.

"You look beautiful." The dress clung to her breasts and put just enough skin on display to tease him and any other guy looking her way. And every time another dude glanced at her, he'd have to resist the urge to rip his arm off, an urge he'd experienced many times while they'd toured the botanical garden. He'd never thought of himself as the jealous type, but each time a guy's eyes lingered on her yesterday, the primitive emotion had reared its head.

"Thank you. Aside from the black eye, you clean up pretty well yourself." She scratched Marley, who had given up on getting any attention from him and started to nudge Kenzie in the shin instead. "My parents should be here soon. They called just before you got here to let me know they were running about ten or fifteen minutes late. I opened a bottle of wine, would you like some? I have a few bottles of beer if you'd rather have that."

A drink, regardless of the kind, would give his hands and mouth something innocent to do while they waited. Maybe it'd even take the edge off whatever emotion he was feeling. Ryan refused to acknowledge he was nervous. He helped bring down dangerous crime lords and protected clients from people who wanted them dead. Meeting his girlfriend's parents was no big deal. "I'll have a glass of wine."

Less than fifteen minutes later, Marley took off from his spot near the back door in the kitchen where he'd been sunning himself. A moment or two later, the doorbell rang, and he added his voice to the announcement that someone was at the door.

Kenzie put the glass she'd picked up back down on the counter. "Be right back."

Thanks to the open floor plan, he could watch as she left the kitchen and walked across the living room. Like a moth drawn to a flame, his eyes zoned in on her ass and the way her dress clung to it as she walked.

Picking up his glass, he swallowed his final mouthful of wine and transferred his gaze from Kenzie's backside to a much safer object, her dog. Satisfied he'd checked on who was at the front door, Marley headed back toward him in search of a little attention.

"Happy birthday. Sorry, we're late. We got a later start than we intended." The deep baritone voice tugged at Ryan's memory, and he looked over toward the door. The man hugging Kenzie appeared a little older, but no question about it, he'd been one of Ryan's firearms instructors at the academy.

Talk about a small world. At least it wasn't the instructor he'd had for defensive tactics. While Kenzie's father had been one of the tougher firearms instructors there, he'd treated all the new agents in training with respect, and he'd been willing to give anyone extra help. The same couldn't be said about the agent in charge of teaching defensive tactics. The man had been an absolute dick. Until this moment, he'd seen none of his instructors again after graduation.

Kenzie immediately made introductions when she came back in the kitchen. "Mom, Dad, this is Ryan." Rather than assign him a label, she looked over at him. "Ryan, my parents, Ed and Maeve."

An older version of Kenzie but with hazel-colored eyes extended her hand toward him. "I'd say it's nice to finally meet you, but until this morning I didn't know Kenzie had someone special in her life." She sent an accusing look in her daughter's direction. "But I'm glad you could join us tonight. I look forward to getting to know you."

Although he was in Edward Armstrong's crosshairs, he focused all his attention on Kenzie's mom. "Thanks for including me."

Maeve appeared about to speak, and if he had to guess, she planned to ask how long he'd known Kenzie, but she never got the opportunity.

"Do you want a glass of wine, Mom?"

"That's Kenzie's way of preventing me from embarrassing her any further." Mother and daughter might look alike, but they didn't sound it. Although not strong, the older woman's voice contained enough of an Irish accent to tell him she'd lived in the United States for a long time, but she hadn't been born here. "We'll talk more later," she promised, patting his shoulder and then stepping away. "I'd love a small glass."

With his wife out of the way, Kenzie's father didn't hesitate to occupy the space she'd vacated. Tall and muscular, Ryan's former firearms instructor wasn't someone you'd want to mess with in a dark alley. The only signs the guy was on the older side were the considerable streaks of gray in his hair and the laugh lines around his mouth. Although retired, he kept himself in excellent shape.

"You look familiar," he said after they shook hands and exchanged greetings. "But I don't know from where."

"Quantico." Ryan stifled the urge to add *sir* to his

response. He was no longer a new agent in training, and he wasn't addressing his instructor.

Ed considered Ryan's answer before nodding. "Saltarelli. Everyone in your class called you Salty. You were at the academy when I was there on a temporary duty assignment. It's good to see you again."

With the mystery of how he knew Ryan solved, Kenzie's dad turned his attention toward his daughter and wife. "If we're going to make our reservation, we should leave soon."

SIX

As much as he loved steak, Ryan preferred throwing a filet or T-bone on the grill and then enjoying it with a cold beer while in the comfort of his own home. That being said, the Fleming Grill was well-known for their steak and seafood, and if he couldn't cook it himself, he wouldn't find a better place to get it. He'd visited the restaurant located in an old bank building built in the early 1920s twice, once when his grandparents stopped to visit on their way to Florida the previous winter and then again when his younger sister came to town. He enjoyed his meals both times. He didn't expect to be disappointed tonight.

Ryan enjoyed the appetizer while he listened to Maeve catch her daughter up on family news. Kenzie might not have any siblings, but the number of cousins, aunts, and uncles she had made up for it. Once Kenzie's mom exhausted that topic, she started on her and Ed's upcoming trip to Ireland in the late fall. As he'd guessed from her accent, she had been born in Ireland and lived there until she was fourteen. Although her parents had moved the family to the United States, Maeve still had many relatives living in Ireland, including a sister who had moved back there not long after graduating from high school.

"Have you thought any more about coming with your dad and me? Everyone would love to see you," Maeve said.

"A three-week vacation isn't possible right now." Kenzie added another seared scallop to her plate before passing the dish to him. As tasty as they were, he'd already enjoyed his share of the appetizer, and with this being their first meeting, he didn't want to look like a gluttonous pig in front of her parents. Rather than set it down, he offered it to Kenzie's mom without taking another helping.

"You don't have to stay as long as we are, and it might still be possible to get on our flight. Faye has the room. When I last spoke to her, she told me to pass along that you're more than welcome to stay with her instead of at a hotel."

"I'm not making any promises, but I'll think about it."

Satisfied at least for the moment with her daughter's response, Maeve moved their conversation on to a cousin of Kenzie's in New York who was due to give birth any day. With both women otherwise engaged, Ryan once again found himself on the receiving end of Ed's full attention, making him feel as if he was about to face an interrogation.

Ed helped himself to another portion of both appetizers, then he offered Ryan another crab cake before starting his questions. Much like with the scallops, he'd already enjoyed his fair share, so he passed even though he would have loved to down two or three more.

"What squad were you assigned to after graduation?" Kenzie's dad asked.

While the academy employed some full-time instructors like the dickhead in charge of defensive tactics, they also cycled in agents certified in various areas to teach for a month or two at a time from the field offices. That had been the case for Edward Armstrong. However, his temporary duty assignment—or TDY—as a firearms instructor had ended before they announced squad and office assignments.

"Spent two years working violent crimes in Phoenix, and then I accepted a transfer to Puerto Rico and did some of that before going to work on the counterterrorism squad." He hadn't been a big fan of Phoenix, but every so often he missed Puerto Rico. Hurricanes aside, the weather had been terrific and the beaches gorgeous.

Ed nodded as he cut his crab cake in half. "Spent some time working violent crimes when I first joined the Bureau. What about now? Are you working at headquarters or are you at the office in Manassas?"

Given what Ed knew about him and where he called home, the question was a logical one, since those two offices were within commuting distance to Dumfries. "I left the FBI about two years ago." Ryan didn't expect Kenzie's father to understand his decision to make a change so soon into his career. After all, the man had spent much of his life working the same job he'd walked away from.

Except for the slight quirk of an eyebrow, Ed's expression didn't change. Regardless, Ryan anticipated his next question and answered it before he asked. "The job wasn't exactly what I expected, and after a while, I got fed up with some aspects of it."

"It's not for everyone. And there is a lot of BS that goes on. You're not the first person I've known to say enough is enough and move on. Considered it once or twice myself at different points in my career."

The conversation between Kenzie and her mom came to a sudden stop. "Really, I didn't know that. I thought you loved working for the Bureau. You used to even go to high school career days and talk about what you did," Kenzie said.

Pushing his empty plate off to the side, Ed transferred his attention to his daughter. "It's like any other job. Some days you love it, and others you want to tell your supervisor what you really think of him and clean out your desk. Thankfully, those days didn't happen too frequently for me, but it's one of the reasons Reggie went into the Legat program. If he hadn't gotten the position, he would've retired around the same time I transferred down here."

"Even I had one of those days two weeks ago, and you know how much I enjoy what I do," Maeve commented, handing the waitress her empty appetizer plate. "But the bride at the last wedding I covered was impossible to work with, and her mother was even worse. I think the father of the bride spent as much time away from the two of them as possible."

Ed dropped his hands in his lap and turned his gaze back in Ryan's direction while a second waitress set down his entrée. "Where do you work now?"

Anyone could go on the internet and find the official website for Elite Force Security. Other than those employed at the top level of management, the site didn't provide a directory of every person who worked there. Ryan, as well as the other members of HRT, were discreet about whom they told that they were part of the organization, so he waited until both restaurant employees left before answering. "I've been with Elite Force Security since leaving the Bureau."

"I've heard of the firm. It has an excellent reputation."

Considering their career choices and similar personalities, she'd expected her dad and Ryan to hit it off. But never in a million years would she have imagined they'd not only previously met, but that her dad had been one of Ryan's instructors. From the little her dad shared about his time teaching, she knew the new agents in training and the instructors at Quantico didn't socialize. Now, though, they completely breached whatever line they'd been unable to cross back then. While she kept a steady conversation going with her mom, her dad and Ryan discussed everything from recent assignments he'd handled for the security firm to which handgun was the best for home protection. By the time the four of them returned to Kenzie's house, anyone seeing the two men together would assume they were old friends. It was a much different scenario from the handful of times her parents and her last boyfriend spent any time together, which honestly hadn't happened much.

Although her mom and dad were always polite to Cullen, she'd always gotten the vibe from them that they wanted to tell him to either disappear or at least shut up. Hell, on occasion even she'd wanted to tell him to shut his trap. After she dumped him, both her parents had separately shared they'd known Cullen wasn't right for her but hadn't wanted to say anything. It was an entirely different story tonight. In fact, she half expected them to invite Ryan along on their trip to Ireland in the fall—a trip she'd love to take with her parents. She'd seen Aunt Faye and a few of her other relatives within the past five years, but the last time she'd visited Ireland had been between her junior and senior years of college. Before she committed to such a vacation, she needed to first see if it was even possible to get the dates off from work. Usually, she put her request in for week-long vacations several months in advance. Her parents' trip was in late October. She also needed to price out flights and decide if the cost and length of the flight were worth it, since she'd only be able to spend at most seven days there. Both tasks she'd handle tomorrow when she took her lunch break.

Since their return to the house, Marley had been going around to each of them looking for attention. For the past ten minutes or so, he'd been getting it from Ryan. When Ryan stood though, disturbing the dog who was currently using his leg as a pillow, Marley gave him what she could only describe as a dog's best attempt at a dirty look.

"I need to go. I have an early morning tomorrow. Thank you again for including me tonight." Ryan extended his hand toward her mom, but she was having none of that tonight. Instead, she came to her feet and did something she never did when Kenzie's ex left: she hugged him.

"It was wonderful to meet you. Ed and I will be in New York for four or five days, and then we're going to head back down to Virginia Beach for a couple more days. If you and Kenzie are free, maybe you can come and spend a night or two with us."

"As long as I'm not working, I'd love to." After returning the embrace, Ryan extended his hand toward her dad. Her dad didn't ignore it and go in for a hug like her mom. The only people he hugged beside her and her mom were female relatives. "Nice to see you again, Ed."

With the formal goodbyes out of the way, Kenzie slipped her hand into Ryan's. "I'll be right back." Except for the short time before her parents arrived, she'd shared Ryan all evening. Before they called it a day—or a night, since it was well after ten o'clock—she wanted another few minutes alone with him, because the last thing she wanted was two sets of parental eyes watching when they said their goodnights.

Like a good little chaperone, Marley followed them out the front door. Unlike her parents, she could deal with him being around.

No sooner did the door close, providing them with some much-appreciated privacy, than Ryan settled his arms around her and pulled her against him. "I have no idea what time I'll be home tomorrow. I'm stopping by Spike's house to visit his parents and sister before they head home." Brushing his lips across hers, he prevented Kenzie from answering. "If it's not too late when I get back, I'd love to see you."

This time he slipped his tongue inside when she parted her lips to answer. The feel of it moving against hers immediately brought to mind her earlier daydream and how he'd used that particular organ on another part of her body. It was in her best interest to push aside the images for the moment. Unfortunately, her mind and body had much different ideas, and neither seemed to care what was best for her sanity or internal temperature.

You cannot ditch your parents and skip over to his house for a quickie. Although the longer he kissed her, the harder she found it to remember why it would be a terrible idea tonight. So before she tossed aside all the manners ever instilled in her and sprinted over to Ryan's house, Kenzie forced her lips to abandon Ryan's.

"My only plan for after work is planting some new flowers in the back. So call me when you get home."

"I will." The erection pressing against her belly spelled out the fact he suffered from the same affliction as she did. Perhaps that explained why he only gave her a kiss worthy of a thirteen-year-old rather than some full tongue action before walking away.

Her mom remained in the same spot, sipping her watermelon-lemon-flavored herbal tea, a flavor Kenzie only kept on hand for when her mom visited, and checking something on her cell phone. She set the device aside as soon as Kenzie retook her seat on the sofa. Marley didn't hesitate to jump up next to her. With his previous pillow gone, he settled his head on her leg instead.

"Where did Dad go?"

"The bathroom. He'll be right back." Her mom's eyes never strayed from Kenzie's face as she took another sip of tea. Whether or not intentional, it felt as if her mom was trying to read her thoughts, and Kenzie just hoped her face didn't reflect the heat still warming her from the inside out thanks to Ryan's mouth and her vivid imagination.

After an eon or two, she set her tea aside. "Ryan seems very nice. I really like him."

It might not sound like it, but coming from her mom, that was a huge compliment. Her mom never announced she liked anyone just to be polite. If she said it, she truly meant it. At the same time, she rarely said anything negative about a person either. Instead, she preferred to operate under the old adage "If you don't have anything nice to say, don't say anything at all."

Me too.

"I'm surprised you didn't tell me about him sooner. How long have you been together?"

Her mom's surprise was understandable. While they didn't talk daily, unless one of them was on vacation, a week never went by that they didn't communicate. While she never shared the intimate details about her relationships, she let her mom know when she was involved with someone.

"We've been spending time together for about the past two weeks, but I've known him since he moved in next door last year. Actually, he moved in not long after I did."

The sound of the bathroom door opening reached them. A moment later, her dad called out. "Do you mind if I find myself a snack?"

"Help yourself."

"While you're in there, can you put more water on for me?" her mom asked before looking back at her. "Well, I have a good feeling about him."

It made no logical sense, but when her mom had a feeling about something, whether it be good or bad, it was usually spot-on. Kenzie hoped this didn't turn out to be the one time her mom wasn't right.

Keith took a gulp of the extra-strong iced coffee he'd purchased at the airport coffee shop and brought up the internet browser on his cell phone. Normally, he used it mostly to either find the results of his favorite sports teams or to check the weather. Since the phone call from his sister yesterday, he'd logged on countless times to check baseball scores but also to view media sites, both the reputable ones and the not so reputable. They confirmed what Jen had shared and what he was still having a difficult time getting his head around. His baby sister was dating his longtime army buddy, Brett Sherbrooke. He wasn't angry that they were involved. Brett was one of the most decent guys he knew. Not that she ever would, but if Jen ever asked him to set her up with one of his friends, Brett would be at the top of his list of potential boyfriends. That aside, it irked him that not once in the almost two years Brett and Jen had been communicating with each other had either bothered to tell him.

Like last night, pictures of Brett alone and some of him and Jen together appeared on every news site he checked out, regardless of how accurate the articles they printed. In high school, he'd played the protective older brother and advised her which guys to stay clear of because they weren't worth her time. Aside from that, he wasn't in the habit of giving her relationship advice. She was a grown adult capable of making her own decisions. Besides, if he ever tried to tell her how to conduct her romantic life, she'd view it as permission to stick her nose into his. He got enough of that from their happily married sister, Kristen. Keith didn't need it from Jen too. But he hoped she'd thought this one through.

Brett was a great guy, but unfortunately, his family name attracted attention around the world. While in the army, he'd been able to fly under the media's radar and live like an average Joe, but now that he was running for a seat in the Senate, the press would be circling him like a vulture around a dead carcass. The media wouldn't only focus on Brett and the Sherbrooke family either. Jen and Brett's relationship would be put under a spotlight too. The pictures posted this weekend were just the beginning. No damn way would he be able to handle the invasion of privacy, and Keith wasn't sure Jen would be able to either. If he had a chance tomorrow, he'd call and see how she was holding up.

His curiosity satisfied, for the time being, Keith switched over to a sports site for the score from the Boston/Los Angeles game and pulled out one of the chocolate-frosted brownies he'd grabbed along with his coffee. Although her plane had just landed according to the screens, his thoughts reverted to the recipient of the second bakery item. Not that it surprised him. Maddie seemed to infiltrate his thoughts regularly these days. It was the worst though on the weekends, when he knew she might be off screwing some faceless dude she met at a bar—not that he had any evidence she ever left bars with random guys—or a man she met through a friend. Maddie might not originally be from the area, but she had a countless supply of friends, both male and female, who loved to set her up with guys. Despite her friends' best efforts, Maddie never seemed to fall for any of the men. A few got multiple dates, but none ever had their phone number stay in Maddie's contact list for more than a month. He knew most didn't even get added to it, because she was almost as open about her romantic life as the rest of the members of the team.

Since he and the rest of HRT knew so much about her private life, it also meant she knew a damn lot about his. Until a couple of months ago, he hadn't cared. Lately, he wished he'd kept his big trap shut rather than talk about what hot piece of ass he'd taken home with him. The fact that she did know a lot about his sex life was only one of the reasons he hesitated every time he thought about crossing the line that friends shouldn't cross. He'd only known Maddie and everyone on the team for about a year and a half, but he considered them family. Sleeping with her could jeopardize not only his friendship with her but with the rest of HRT too. When faced with a potentially dangerous situation, he liked having as much information as possible before making any move. Although not dangerous in the same way, before he took the first step over the friendship line, he'd like to have more intel.

Yeah, sure, Maddie considered him a friend. They hung out occasionally, and she happily busted his balls every chance she got. However, except for Ax, their supervisor, Maddie hung out with all the guys on the team. Nothing she ever said or did suggested she viewed him any differently.

"Hey, I hope you grabbed me one of those."

Great situational awareness, moron. He'd learned early in his military career to always know who and what was around him, because it could mean the difference between life and death. The same was true in his current line of work. Yet, he'd had his head so far up his own ass just now he didn't realize Maddie had entered the coffee shop they agreed to meet in until she spoke.

Keith pushed the bag across the table. "Grabbed you an iced coffee too."

With no hesitation, she pulled out the brownie and took a long sip of her drink. "You're a lifesaver. I could kiss you for getting me this."

Go right ahead. "Anytime."

She lifted the cup toward her mouth again, and his eyes refused to look away as her lips closed around the luckiest piece of plastic in the world. Damn, what he wouldn't give to have her lips close around him right now.

The vivid image of Maddie pleasuring him filled his head,

and Keith reached for his drink, extremely glad mind reading wasn't possible. If it were, there was a good chance he'd be wearing the contents of the cup in Maddie's hand.

"Do you need to stop anywhere before we head over to baggage claim?" The first pit stop he made after a flight was the restroom. Airplane bathrooms were a complete joke, and he avoided them at all costs.

"I only used a carry-on." She pointed to the bag near her feet. "So I'm ready to leave whenever you are."

Keith had thought he traveled light. "You didn't take much."

"We spent most of our time either on the beach or at the hotel pool."

He'd never seen Maddie in anything skimpier than running shorts and a tank top. The lack of a visual reference didn't stop his brain from inventing an image of her in a fire-engine red bikini as they exited the building.

"What about you? What did you do this weekend? Or maybe I should say who did you do this weekend?" Maddie asked.

"Spent some time at the gym with Spike and Salty, but otherwise I hung out at home watching the ballgames and stuff."

She sent him a *yeah right* look. "You spent the weekend alone?"

Yep, he wished he'd been a little more discreet about sharing information in the past. "Something wrong with that?" She made it sound like he couldn't go a single weekend without having a woman over.

"No. It just seems like you don't spend much time alone on your days off."

She wasn't wrong. His weekends a few months ago were much different than his recent ones. But, of course, she had no way of knowing that. Other than Spike and Salty, no one knew his sex life was nonexistent at the moment, thanks to his inability to make a move when it came to Maddie.

Using the key fob, Keith unlocked his SUV and got behind the wheel. "There wasn't anyone I wanted to spend time with."

"What happened to Lisa?" Maddie dropped her bag on the floor and then fastened her seat belt.

They'd had some fun together, but these days Lisa was a distant memory. "I haven't seen her in a few months."

"Really? Since you haven't mentioned anyone else, I thought maybe things were getting serious between you two. I should have known better. You have an aversion to relationships that might lead somewhere, like my brother."

On the positive side, she'd noticed he hadn't been talking about a different woman every other week. Unfortunately, she thought he was afraid of commitment, which he wasn't. It was more a case of finding no one he cared enough about to give it a try.

Out of the corner of his eye, he watched her take another sip of iced coffee. "The only thing I have an aversion to are oysters." For the most part, he loved seafood, but he could never get past the sight of oysters to even try them.

"Whatever you say." There was a trace of laughter in her voice. "I saw several pictures of a woman who looks like your sister and Brett Sherbrooke together. Was it Jen?"

At the moment, he saw no way to convince Maddie she was wrong about him, so he wasn't going to waste his breath and try. But he'd figure out something. "Yeah," he answered and then explained how his sister and the billionaire met.

SEVEN

After locking his desk drawer, Gabe shoved his cell phone in his back pocket and grabbed his gym bag off the floor. Since most of the guys he trained didn't even get to the gym until six or seven, he usually stuck around until the place closed most nights. However, if he was being honest with himself, he didn't only stay so late every night because he had clients to train. Unlike his younger brother, he didn't have anyone waiting at home for him. Instead, he had frozen dinners and his best friend, a bottle of eighteen-year-old scotch. Sticking around the gym allowed him to help save his liver while at the same time take his anger out on an unsuspecting punching bag or whoever was unlucky enough to get on the mats with him.

"Hey, Mom wanted me to remind you the party starts at one tomorrow." Xander paused at the open office door. Judging by the bag slung over his shoulder, he was on his way out too.

A brief jab of envy poked Gabe in the vicinity of his heart at the thought of what his baby brother had to look forward to in a little while. Lillian sometimes drove him crazy, and he could never live with her, but she loved Xander and took great care of their three children.

"I'll do my best to stop in."

Every five years the family held a reunion, forcing him to see relatives he didn't care a rat's ass about. The party tomorrow was the last place he wanted to be. No doubt his mom would give him grief if he didn't at least make an appearance. The last time they spoke, she'd insisted showing up and socializing with the family would be a good way to put the past behind him. He knew hearing about how much his aunt's leg bothered her every time it rained or listening to his cousins go on about their kids' accomplishments wouldn't change anything in his life. It certainly wouldn't help put the past several years behind him. Only one thing would help with that. After his meeting with Sam, hopefully he'd be one step closer to settling the score with the man who ruined his life.

Before his baby brother launched into a lecture and regurgitated the spiel his mom already delivered, he walked around the desk and through the door. "I'm heading out. I'll see you later."

Xander didn't take the hint and fell into step alongside him. "A little early for you to be leaving."

Gabe didn't have to explain his comings and goings to Xander. The guy was his brother, not his keeper. But they'd always had a good relationship, and unlike a lot of people, his brother hadn't let Gabe's short prison stint change anything between them.

"Big plans tonight?" Xander pushed open the exit door and held it until Gabe joined him outside.

He knew what kind of plans Xander referred to, and if his brother wanted to believe he was going out with someone,

Gabe wasn't going to tell him any differently. "Yeah, and I'm running late. Say hi to Lillian and the kids." His brother could be worse than a woman sometimes when it came to wanting to know specific details, so before Xander could grill him, he stepped off the curb and headed for his car.

Last week, Sam had come to him for their initial meeting. When Gabe had received the text message from the private investigator yesterday, he offered to meet him at Sam's office this time. Since so many people came and went from the gym every day, there was a good chance no one would remember if Sam stopped by more than once, but Gabe saw no reason to tempt fate. Besides, Sam's office wasn't far from the gym.

Unlike with the other doors along the hallway, there was no large plaque or lettering on the door letting visitors know what was located on the other side. There was only the number 225. Opening the door, Gabe stepped inside the nondescript waiting room. There were no paintings on the walls or magazines on tables. A handful of chairs lined one side of the room, and a sliding window on another suggested Sam employed a receptionist or perhaps a personal assistant. At the moment, there was no one seated there. Rather than open the door leading to the rest of the office and find himself on the opposite end of a handgun—he didn't doubt Sam carried one most of the time—he sent off a text message letting the private investigator know he'd arrived.

The door opened a moment or two later. Although the cargo pants and T-shirt were a different color than last week, once again nothing about the guy stood out. "C'mon in." Sam didn't stick around and wait for Gabe to follow him.

Two desks occupied the area on the other side of the glass window. A picture frame and a laptop sat on one, while a vase of fresh flowers and a desktop computer occupied the other, suggesting Sam employed at least two individuals. From what his contacts had shared, he'd assumed Sam handled all aspects of his business, but maybe even private investigators with flexible morals needed people to handle accounting issues and answer the phone.

Sam already sat behind his desk when Gabe walked in. Much like the rest of the office, it contained the bare minimum. "Before I give you the information, I need payment."

He'd expected nothing less. Unzipping his gym bag, Gabe pulled out the envelope he'd removed from his safe earlier this morning. He tried to use cash for as many things as possible. Although Sam accepted other forms of payment, Gabe didn't want a paper trail connecting them.

"Are you sure it's him?" Before he handed over anything, he needed some kind of assurance Sam had the right guy.

Sam's jaw tightened, but he didn't argue. Instead, he slid a manila envelope across the desk. "Check."

Gabe pulled out two 8x10 photos from the envelope. He appeared a few years older, but no question the man smiling up at him from the top one was Special Agent Edward Armstrong.

"Is it him?" Sam asked.

Pain shot up the side of his face, and he forced himself to unclench his teeth as he handed over the money.

"Your buddy isn't working for the FBI anymore. He retired three and a half years ago. He owns a self-defense and firearms school in Woodbridge. According to the website, they provide training to local law enforcement agencies as well as civilians. Armstrong's wife, Maeve, is a local photographer." Sam handed over a computer flash drive. "Everything is on here, including their home address in Springfield and their address in Virginia Beach."

"Any children or grandchildren?"

Sam smirked. "You asked me to locate him and his wife. And I just gave you the information. You want more, I'll find it, but it'll be extra."

He planned to make Armstrong suffer as much as he had. "Let me know when you have the rest." In the meantime, he would review the information Sam had gathered so far and get in contact with Jax and Shawn, two employees of Zane's who occasionally came into the gym to train.

EIGHT

Ryan rolled his neck and reached for the cup of extra-strong coffee he'd grabbed from the kitchen before heading into the team's meeting room for a debrief. If he had any hope of staying awake, not only through the rest of the meeting but for any amount of time when he got home, he needed all the caffeine he could get his hands on. Although honestly, he cared far more about being alert when he got home than he did about the rest of this meeting. He had no doubt Kenzie would understand if he passed out the second they sat down. Thanks to a crazy week, they'd exchanged several text messages, but he'd only been able to spend about an hour with her all week, and that had been Tuesday morning. If he'd known what a busy week it would turn into, he would've skipped his visit with Spike's family Monday night, a visit that had lasted far longer than he intended.

When he walked into Spike's house, he planned to catch up a little, promise to visit Mr. and Mrs. Brockman the next time he was in New Hampshire, and head out. His plans took a detour when Audrey, Spike's little sister, walked in the kitchen. To his shock and something bordering on horror, a beautiful young woman who would have guys studying her rather than their books had replaced the baby-faced beanpole with braces he remembered from two Christmases ago. Although she wasn't his sister, Ryan's older-brother instincts kicked in and immediately he found himself singing the praises of Georgetown and all the area universities Audrey had visited over the weekend. If Spike's sister went to a college in the D.C. area, they could both keep an eye on her and be nearby if she ever needed any kind of help. Before he did finally leave, Spike's father pulled him aside and thanked him for his efforts. Whether they'd helped sway Audrey's decision was anyone's guess.

Since he'd gotten home so late Monday night, they met for breakfast Tuesday morning at a restaurant about halfway between Parkview Immediate Care, the clinic where Kenzie worked, and Elite Force's headquarters. Despite plans to get together later that same evening, it never happened. He'd barely taken three steps off the elevator at work before Ax called him in his office and handed him a plane ticket to Florida. Unless the assignment was for a high-value client, like the Sherbrookes or Stan Bonds, protection assignments went to one of the firm's well-trained bodyguards rather than to a member of HRT, leaving the team free to carry out the firm's other responsibilities. Responsibilities that very few people knew Elite Force even had—the firm, the federal government, and local law enforcement preferred it that way. Unfortunately, Stephan Berkeley was the son of an English aristocrat who happened to be close friends with Hugh Allen, the firm's CFO. So rather than send someone else to babysit the arrogant jerk while he partied in Miami, Ryan got stuck with the task. After meeting Stephan at the airport, he'd spent the next few days more or less protecting the nineteen-year-old from himself until his father and mother arrived late Thursday night. As soon as he handed over the reins to a man who turned out to be the complete opposite of his son in both looks and personality, Ryan hopped a red-eye flight home. Somehow he managed to sneak in four hours of sleep before heading into work this morning. He'd been running on caffeine and sugar ever since. Exhausted or not, Ryan would not let it stop him from spending time with Kenzie tonight. But first, he had to make it through the rest of this never-ending debriefing.

"Salty, do you have anything to add?" Ax asked, putting a temporary halt to the images running through Ryan's head depicting how he hoped the night would end.

Honestly, he had almost no idea what Neil had already shared. He'd tuned out a good ten minutes ago. There wasn't a chance in hell he would admit that. "No."

Several months ago, Elite Force had been contacted by the parents of a teenage girl from Virginia who was lured away from home by a violent Baltimore-based organization that'd been pimping out girls as young as fourteen while also making sure the drug problem in the city continued. Almost immediately the firm partnered with the local authorities to get all the girls safely home and at the same time eradicate the organization. With no hesitation, Neil Foley had volunteered to go undercover. Today he'd had another meeting with the organization's second-in-command, meaning Ryan and Keith had spent much of the day inside a run-down apartment in an unsavory neighborhood listening to Neil's wire in case he needed backup. Although an essential and often beneficial assignment, it was also the one they all dreaded because it was boring as hell. Well, unless something went wrong, and then the adrenaline kicked in. Today the meeting had gone as Neil hoped.

"What about you?" Ax directed his question across the table to Keith this time.

Keith shook his head as he checked his watch again. He

hadn't shared his plans with Ryan; actually, he'd been unusually quiet today despite the hours they'd spent together. But whatever they were, the guy was eager to leave. He'd looked at his watch at least three times in the last fifteen minutes.

"Then we're done here. Neil, let me know the next time you're in contact with Roche."

Thank God. He liked the people he worked with and what he did, but he'd had enough of both for the week.

"I'm heading over to Cooper's Smokehouse. Either of you interested?" Neil asked, pushing his chair away from the conference table.

He often stopped at the barbeque joint in Alexandria after work for dinner and a beer. Any other night, he'd take Neil up on the offer. "Not tonight. I already have plans."

"Next-door neighbor again?" Keith asked.

Ryan nodded as he sent Kenzie a text message letting her know he was leaving work soon and should be home in about a half an hour so she could come over whenever she wanted.

Neil grabbed his cell phone and stuck it in a back pocket. "The one that came to your cookout? Thought about asking her for her number, but after the way you kept looking at her all night, I got the feeling you were interested in her. Any plans tonight, Keith?"

"Sorry, I'm meeting some friends. See you both later." Keith didn't elaborate or stick around for any questions.

Friends or a friend? Maybe Keith had finally grown a set and asked Maddie out. If he had, it would explain his eagerness to leave tonight. Ryan preceded Neil into the hallway. "Have a nice weekend. See you on Monday." At least he hoped he didn't see Neil or anyone else until Monday. Unfortunately, in this line of work, there were no guarantees.

"Yeah, you too."

Ryan stopped at his desk long enough to grab his keys,

and then he split before anyone decided a late Friday afternoon conversation was a good idea.

The perfect evening for a ride in his convertible greeted him outside. He hadn't checked the weather for the rest of the weekend, but he hoped they were in store for more of the same. After being stuck inside an apartment that reeked of fish and old cigarettes for much of the day, he wanted fresh air and plenty of it. So rather than use the car's air conditioning, Ryan put all the windows down and pulled up a playlist on his cell phone before heading out of the gated parking lot.

He was less than a block from work when the guitar riff from one of his favorite songs interrupted the chorus coming from the speakers. A glance at the screen confirmed it was a call he wanted to take and not another of the endless junk calls he, like most people, received daily.

"Hey, Adam. What's up?" It'd been at least a week since he last talked to his brother.

"I'm heading up to see Mom and Dad this weekend." His twin brother's voice, which he was told sounded exactly like his, came through the car's speakers.

Damn it. He didn't need to hear anything else. Adam had a key to his house, and when he was in the area, he came and went as he pleased. The same was true in Ryan's case, although he traveled down to North Carolina much less than Adam came to Virginia. If his brother was driving north, he planned to spend the night at his place. Usually, Ryan enjoyed having his brother around. Tonight wasn't one of those times.

"But I'm at your place now. Just checking if you're on an assignment or if you'll be around tonight."

Anyone else, he'd tell them to get lost. He'd even consider telling one of his other two brothers that tonight, but not Adam. While he had great relationships with both Kyle and Ben, they were nothing like the one between him and his twin. So telling Adam to find another place to sleep tonight wasn't an option, regardless of what his dick was telling him.

"On my way home now. I'd tell you to make yourself at home, but I know you already did." Ryan ended the call before Adam could get in a comeback.

His brother had the worst timing. Although he didn't need to change his plans for the night, an overnight visitor meant he had to alter them. Earlier in the week, Kenzie had understood when he'd been forced to change their plans. Ryan hoped she remained that way tonight.

Crazy or not, she never left the house without saying goodbye to Marley—and Silver, if the cat was around. More times than not, Silver was off somewhere in the house happy to be alone, and occasionally Kenzie envied the cat for her ability to do that. If Kenzie had to guess, the cat was upstairs at the moment in her bedroom, soaking up some sun. She'd most likely stay there as long as the sun did; then she'd find her way to the kitchen and nibble on her food.

"Be a good boy." Kenzie scratched Marley behind the ears, and in return, he looked at her as if she was about to abandon him forever. "Don't look at me like that. I'll be back soon."

Unconvinced by the words, he followed her to the front door. "It won't work tonight, buddy." On occasion, she took him with her when she left. Regardless of whether or not Ryan would welcome the dog into his house, she didn't want a third wheel, even if it would be a furry one, around tonight. She doubted Ryan would want one either. The little time they'd spent together so far this week had been inside a busy restaurant. Not exactly the type of place where one could get up close and personal, and tonight she wanted to get as close and personal as humanly possible. She didn't expect to get any disagreements from Ryan's corner either.

Kenzie scooted out the door before Marley's pleading puppy dog eyes changed her mind about bringing him along, because when it came to him, she was a big softy. He seemed to know it too.

The dark blue convertible parked in front of Ryan's house caused an odd combination of disappointment and annoyance to settle in her stomach. They hadn't discussed any specific plans for tonight or really the weekend except for the Nationals game tomorrow. However, she'd assumed they'd be alone. If he planned to have other friends over, it would have been nice if he'd let her know in advance. Nothing in his texts this week suggested anyone else would be here.

She was near the edge of her driveway when Ryan's front door opened and he jogged down the steps, causing her feet to slow as a burst of heat cascaded over her, forcing any other emotion aside. He might have a friend over now, but they wouldn't stay the night. Eventually, they'd go home, and the two of them would have the rest of the night to enjoy each other's company in ways that involved very little conversation and no clothing. At least she hoped that was how they'd be spending part of their time together.

Picking up her pace, she met him in the middle of his driveway. While they were alone, she wanted to give him a proper greeting. Stepping closer to him, she slipped her arms over his shoulders and pressed her body against his. "I missed—"

Pushing away from him, Kenzie studied his face. The man in front of her looked like Ryan, but at the same time, he didn't. She couldn't explain it. But something was off.

"You—" Ryan didn't finish whatever he intended to say because behind him the door banged closed.

"Hey, Kenzie. I was just coming over to get you."

At the sound of Ryan's voice, she glanced past the Ryan standing in front of her, whom she'd almost kissed, and watched a second one head in her direction.

Heat crawled up her neck as Kenzie eyes swung back for another glimpse at who must be Adam. Ryan had told her he had a twin brother, but nothing he said suggested they were identical, and no family pictures were hanging on his walls to tell her. And thanks to the lack of information, she'd almost kissed Adam while standing in his brother's driveway.

Despite the audience, Ryan tugged her against him and covered her mouth with his without a word to his brother. The movement of his lips against hers quickly sent any embarrassment into hiding for the moment, and a fresh dose of desire swept over her.

"I missed you this week." He whispered the words against her ear before tugging gently on her earlobe.

An exaggerated throat clearing reminded Kenzie they weren't alone. Considering the fact Ryan had transferred his lips from her ear to her neck, he was content to ignore his brother and continue with what he was doing. If they were alone, she wouldn't object at all to Ryan's current activity. But having him tease her while another man with the same face, whom she'd hugged, looked on was simply too weird for her.

Taking a step back, she moved out of Ryan's embrace and looked in Adam's direction. She'd almost kissed the man, so he deserved at least an apology. For all she knew, Adam had a girlfriend or fiancée inside the house. Even if it was a mistake, she wouldn't be too happy to walk outside and find another woman kissing Ryan because she thought he was his brother. "I'm sorry about that."

Adam grinned, something Ryan had done many times around her, and when he did, she often wished for a place to sit down. But although their features were the same, she didn't fear her legs would give out.

"Don't worry about. It happens a lot," Adam replied.

She hoped he meant people confused them a lot rather than the wrong women kissed them a lot. "I knew Ryan had a twin. But I didn't know you were identical." She shot Ryan a look of annoyance. "If I'd known, I think I would have realized you were Adam sooner." The longer she looked at Adam, the more she picked up the subtle differences, such as the tiny scar near Adam's right eye and the slight difference in their hair length.

She'd more or less thrown herself at the man, so shaking his hand seemed silly. Regardless, she extended her hand toward him. "It's nice to meet you."

"I think we're past handshakes, Kenzie." Adam wrapped an arm around her and kissed her cheek, ignoring the glare Ryan sent his way. Nodding in Ryan's direction, he dropped his hands by his sides. "Considering the way he's looking at me, maybe I better sleep with a knife under my pillow tonight."

If Ryan were giving her a look like the one he was giving his brother, she'd be running for cover. "Might not be a bad idea."

Ryan's arm went around her waist, and he pulled her back against his side. Unlike earlier, she wouldn't be able to get away from him easily. Not that she wanted to anyway. She'd spent more time this week than was probably healthy thinking about him and how they could spend their time together.

"I thought you were leaving to get some food," Ryan said.

Although it was obvious to anyone with ears that Ryan wanted him gone, Adam ignored his brother. "Is he this rude to you? Because if he is, I'll take care of it for you. It wouldn't be the first time I had to teach him some manners."

"He's thoughtful around me." She could pull out a whole

list of other adjectives but saw no need to. The little glint in Adam's eyes let her know the single word was all the ammunition he required.

"Thoughtful?" He shook his head in disbelief. "Ryan doesn't know the meaning of the word. Are you sure you're not thinking of thoughtless? Or maybe tedious? People have used both words to describe my baby brother here."

Her lips twitched, and it took some effort, but she contained a smile. "Positive."

Adam glanced at his brother before focusing his attention back on her, and she couldn't help but wonder what it was like to look at a person with the same face as you. Was it like looking in a mirror? Or did they know each other so well that they saw more the person inside rather than what the rest of the world saw?

"Sorry, Kenzie, I know my brother, and I'm not buying it. We'll talk when I get back."

She had a feeling they would, and in the process, she'd get to hear every embarrassing story Adam could think of about his brother. Kenzie didn't doubt Ryan would repay the favor. If nothing else, it would be an entertaining and perhaps informative night.

"Take the long way home," Ryan called over his shoulder as he started to walk them across the driveway toward the front steps, leaving Adam behind.

Letting him know how much she would have appreciated knowing he and Adam were identical twins was on the tip of her tongue, because she wasn't in the habit of throwing herself at men. The fact that she'd just done so was perhaps the most embarrassing thing she'd done in her adult life. Before she could tell him that or anything else, he closed the door behind them and slammed his lips down on hers. Seconds later, his hands tugged the elastic holding her hair up in a ponytail and he backed her up against the door, trapping her there with his body.

Labeling what he was doing to her mouth a kiss was wrong. Unfortunately, her brain couldn't come up with an adequate word. And when he moved his lips away from hers, it was like a giant had snuffed out all the sunlight in the world. Like a little child, she wanted to stomp her feet and demand that he return to what he'd been doing.

"Sorry I was so busy this week," he said between kisses against her neck. Ryan pulled a handful of her shirt free from her waistband and touched the bare skin underneath. Slowly, his hand skimmed up her stomach before settling on her breast.

"I—" Kenzie sucked in air as his thumb flicked across her nipple, and he smiled against her neck. "—understand."

And she did. Some jobs followed a set schedule and allowed people to make plans not only days in advance but weeks. Others, though, changed daily and forced you, as well as those in your life, to be flexible and understanding. His job was one of those, and she didn't expect or need any apology.

Ryan's other hand sneaked under her shirt and released the clip between her breasts holding her bra closed. Like he had on the outside, he flicked his thumb across her taut nipple, intensifying the ache already building between her legs.

If he planned to get her all hot and bothered, she would repay the favor. Maneuvering her hand between their bodies, she freed the button on his cargo pants and slipped a hand inside. Kenzie traced the head of his erection with her fingertip, eliciting a groan from Ryan.

Closing her hand around him, she gradually slid her hand down the length of him, his skin soft and hot against her palm. "How long do you think Adam will be gone?" She'd been thinking about Ryan naked and inside her for much of the week. If she needed to wait hours for it to happen, she might explode, especially after this little petting session.

With no warning, Ryan yanked her shirt up and over her head. Her bra quickly followed her shirt, and where either landed was anyone's guess. "Long enough." His mouth took the place of his fingers against her nipple.

It was all she needed to hear.

Moving her head off his shoulder, Kenzie propped herself on an elbow and looked at him. Thanks to his fingers, her hair looked like she'd gone through a wind tunnel set at maximum speed. Her hair wasn't the only visual evidence of their recent activities either. Kenzie's lips were red and swollen, and he didn't need to look at his back to know he was sporting some scratches.

"You should have told me you and Adam were identical."

The sight of her naked breasts within arm's reach made it difficult to concentrate on much else. The tone of her voice suggested he better do his best though. Reaching up, he brushed a piece of hair away from her eyes and tucked it behind her ear. "I thought I did."

Honestly, he couldn't say one way or the other. Maybe if they weren't both naked, he could focus on something besides rolling her onto her back and making love to her again. But after what he'd just experienced, it was unlikely to happen. He'd had sex with plenty of women. None of those times compared to what they'd just done.

She shook her head, causing her hair to sway against his chest. "You only mentioned you had a twin." She flopped back down next to him and stared up at the ceiling. "I can't believe I almost kissed him."

"You're not the first person to mistake one of us for the

other. And trust me, Adam wouldn't have minded if you kissed him." But Ryan sure as hell would have, even if it had been an accident.

"It's still embarrassing."

Fear and embarrassment were two emotions he'd stopped feeling a long time ago. Neither served much of a purpose in his opinion, so why bother with either. "Forget about it." Leaning over, he passed his lips across hers and covered her breast with his hand.

Kenzie's hand unexpectedly came down on his, and she turned her face, making it impossible to kiss her. "Did you hear that? I think your brother is back."

If Adam was back, he didn't care. His brother wasn't stupid. When he didn't see them downstairs, he'd know to mind his own business and entertain himself until they got around to joining him. Ryan would do the same if the tables were reversed.

"If he is, so what? We're all adults. He doesn't care what we do." With her mouth turned away from him, he kissed her neck instead.

This time she wiggled away from him and yanked the sheet up, covering her breasts and depriving him of a view he'd love to look at for the rest of the night. "What if he comes up here? The bedroom door is open. I think we should go downstairs."

He couldn't promise Adam wouldn't need something from his bags in the spare bedroom. If his brother walked by the door and caught them in the middle of something, it wouldn't faze Ryan. It wouldn't bother a lot of the women he'd had in his bed either. But if almost kissing Adam had embarrassed Kenzie, he could only imagine how she'd feel if his brother saw them having sex. It would probably embarrass her too if Adam heard her. He didn't know if Kenzie realized it or not, but she wasn't quiet when she came.

Closing his eyes, he rolled onto his back. "You're right."

On the off chance that Adam would come wandering upstairs, Ryan climbed out of bed and closed the door so she could get dressed. "He'll only be here tonight. He's driving up to see our parents. If I'd known his plans, I would have told you, but I didn't. Adam called me on my way home."

Ryan made no move to get dressed; instead, he watched her pull on her underwear and shorts while at the same time thinking about how much he was looking forward to getting both off her again soon.

Bending down, she gifted him with an excellent view of her ass while she searched among the discarded blankets and then under the bed. "Do you know where my shirt and bra are?"

"Downstairs." They'd left both near the front door. His T-shirt was somewhere out in the hall, along with his shoes. "I'll grab you one of my T-shirts."

As he'd expected, Adam hadn't cared they weren't around when he came back. Instead, he'd brought the takeout he'd picked up into the kitchen, grabbed a bottle of sparkling water from the refrigerator, and started eating. He hadn't even bothered to take extra plates from the cupboard for them to use when they joined him.

"Wasn't sure when I'd see you again, so I started without you." He dug into his food without commenting on the clothes he'd passed on his way in the house or the fact Kenzie was wearing one of Ryan's New England Rebels T-shirts.

If Adam's comment bothered her, Kenzie didn't let on. Instead, she pulled out a chair and sat down. "I haven't had Indian food in months. You must have gone to Kashmir. I wish they were a little closer; I'd order from them more often."

Ryan felt the same way. If he was getting takeout, he rarely felt like driving twenty minutes just to pick up the food and another twenty to get home. While the place delivered, he lived outside the radius they'd travel. Unfortunately, it was the only Indian restaurant in their general area. Although tonight the forty-minute round trip to the joint had proved to be a plus. Even with his brother there, they could have disappeared upstairs and enjoyed themselves until Adam left in the morning, but he didn't need Kenzie to tell him that she wouldn't have been comfortable with that. And if he'd had to wait much longer to be inside her, his erection might have become permanent.

Since his brother hadn't been polite enough to set the table for three, Ryan grabbed more plates and snagged two bottles of iced tea. "Thanks for getting dinner."

Adam's slight nod as Kenzie looked over the various selections on the table confirmed he understood Ryan was thanking him for more than buying the food.

"Kenzie, feel free to ask me anything you want about my baby brother, and I'll answer."

Kenzie added several items from the appetizer platter to her plate, along with a spoonful of aloo palak, one of his favorite vegetable dishes from the restaurant, and a large slice of naan bread. "I think I'm good, but if something comes to mind, I'll let you know."

Under the table, she touched Ryan's thigh, and an area in the center of his chest tightened. He'd known from day one that their relationship would differ from his past ones. However, he hadn't expected her to become so important to him this quickly.

NINE

Both the living room and kitchen were empty when Ryan returned. After grabbing a beer from the refrigerator, he followed the music outside.

"I didn't think I'd see you before I left in the morning," Adam greeted from his spot near the fire pit where he'd started a nice blaze.

Kenzie had invited him to spend the night, and he'd considered it because leaving her bed to come home had been damn near impossible. The only reason he'd finally dragged his sorry ass out of the house was because his brother was here and he wasn't sure when he'd see Adam again.

Dropping into a seat, Ryan stretched out his legs and took a swig from his bottle. "She asked me to stay, and I thought about leaving you to fend for yourself. But I knew how crushed you'd be if you didn't see me before you went to bed."

"More like the other way around, bro." Adam took a handful of chips from the bag he held and then passed it to him. "I sure as hell wouldn't have come back if she asked me to stay—well, unless Mom was here."

Ryan's stomach clenched up. *It's Adam.* Even if he was single, which he wasn't, his brother would never make a move on Kenzie.

"I like Kenzie. What made you finally ask her out?" Adam asked.

Even though they'd met for the first time today, he'd mentioned Kenzie to Adam a handful of times over the past year they'd been neighbors. However, he'd never let on he was interested in her, so it was a logical question. It was also a loaded question. One he wasn't sure he wanted to answer with 100 percent honesty, even if it was only Adam sitting there. "I realized a few weeks ago that she was single. If I'd known she dumped her boyfriend months ago, I would've asked her sooner."

The statement was more or less true. She had dumped her boyfriend months ago, but he'd known she was single long before he'd asked her out, which meant he could have made his move long before he did. On some level, he'd known if he got involved with Kenzie, their relationship would be different than any other he'd had. It'd taken him a while to decide that not only was he ready for a different kind of relationship, but it was what he wanted.

"And it took you months to figure out she was single? She lives next door, and you never noticed she didn't have a guy coming over? You're losing your touch. You used to be observant."

There wasn't much that happened in the neighborhood he didn't pick up on. Once he'd determined the same gray Jeep that used to be in her driveway no longer came by, he'd brought up the topic in a casual conversation and learned the vehicle belonged to some jerk named Cullen who she had kicked to the curb. Of course, she hadn't used those specific words, but he was good at reading between the lines.

Ryan shrugged and dropped the bag of chips back on the

table between them. Some comments weren't worth address-ing. "I don't know what time you plan on leaving, but Kenzie invited us both over for breakfast in the morning."

"I'm in no rush." Adam took a drink from his beer and reached for the bag. "I need a woman who will cook me breakfast. Does she do it often?"

"First time."

His brother grinned. "She must want a chance to compare us and make sure she's with the right brother."

Again his stomach clenched up, and he reminded himself Adam was just giving him a hard time—an activity all the Saltarelli children took great pride in.

"I've got time. Maybe I should stick around and cook for her. A nice romantic dinner for two might be the thing to put me in the lead."

"Too late. I did that last weekend," Ryan replied, his lips barely moving. The caveman inside him was having a diffi-cult time letting go of the jealousy his brother's words kept evoking.

Adam's smiled disappeared, and he lowered the bottle back to the small table next to him. "I'm only joking with you. I didn't realize things were so serious between the two of you."

Exhaling a deep breath, he put his beer down too. "Yeah, I know."

"Are you going to take her up to New Hampshire for Thanksgiving or maybe Christmas?"

The holidays were still months away, but he planned on asking her to come along because he wanted Kenzie to meet his family. If she couldn't join him for the holidays, maybe they could make a quick trip up to New Hampshire in the near future. "That's the plan." Ryan dipped his chip in the jar of salsa his brother had brought outside and popped it in his mouth. "Too bad Katie isn't with you this weekend. Mom's eager to meet her. Last time I talked to Mom, she asked if I'd met her yet. Is she teaching summer classes?" His brother had been with Katie, a professor at a community college, for five or six months, and by the way he talked about her, things were getting serious. Still, no one in the family had met her yet.

Following Ryan's lead, Adam scooped up a healthy serving of salsa on his chip and brought it toward his mouth. "We haven't seen each other in over a month."

"What did she do, ask for a ring?" When it came to women, Adam was far pickier than him—or the pre-Kenzie him. His brother didn't do one-night stands. Generally, Adam's relationships lasted months, sometimes even up to a year. Despite his preference for monogamous long-term relationships, Adam called it quits whenever a girlfriend brought up moving in together or marriage, a fact that baffled Ryan, because if you liked someone enough to stay with them for a year, moving in together seemed like a logical next step.

"Nah. She ended it, not me."

In all the years his brother had been dating, Ryan couldn't remember a woman ever giving Adam the boot. But hey, there was a first time for everything. Wasn't he planning to introduce Kenzie to his family, something he hadn't done since college?

"Back in June, one of my cases had me working a lot of crazy hours. And I don't know how many times we had plans and I had to call and tell her I couldn't come by. Then I ended up spending a week in San Diego for one of my cases. Back in July, she told me she was tired of it. She wanted someone who she could depend on being around."

There were no exterior lights on, but the fire gave off enough light to see Adam's face. Despite the end of his relationship, he didn't look or sound upset.

"Kenzie knows what you do, right?" Adam reached over to grab another log for the fire and added it to the flames.

With a mouthful of food, he nodded.

"Do you think she'll be okay with it? You work some strange hours sometimes."

It was a reasonable question, especially considering the reason Katie had left Adam. "Yeah. Her father is a retired FBI agent. I'm sure she experienced him having some crazy work schedules. Even her mom worked for the Bureau as a forensic photographer, so I'm sure she didn't work nine to five either."

Ryan watched the flames dance for a moment and wondered what the probability was that he'd have not only found himself living next door to the daughter of a retired FBI agent but that she'd be the daughter of an instructor he'd had at the academy. Statistics weren't his thing—Kyle was the numbers guy in the family—but even he knew the chances had to be extremely low.

"Do her parents live nearby?"

"Springfield. Kenzie's dad and another former agent own a self-defense and firearms school in Woodbridge. But I met them last weekend."

"Already meeting Mom and Dad? You really do have it bad." Adam took his final mouthful of beer and stood up. "I'm getting another. Do you want me to grab you one?"

He was in no rush to go to bed, and even though they were adults, he still missed spending time with Adam and took advantage of every opportunity he got. "Yeah." Ryan glanced up at his brother long enough to answer. Then he turned his attention back to the fire.

His twin was right. He'd been physically attracted to Kenzie the first time he met her not long after he moved into the neighborhood. It hadn't taken long before her personality captured just as much of his attention. Now she was quickly taking possession of his heart as well.

Maddie watched as her friend Jasmine touched Keith's arm while she finished sharing the details of her most recent trip to Puerto Rico. Jasmine had been doing similar things since the moment she arrived for the friendly poker game and her eyes landed on Keith. While Jasmine was a great friend with many endearing traits, she couldn't be around anyone with a Y chromosome and not flirt. So her behavior tonight wasn't unexpected. Maddie would never admit it to a single soul, but Jasmine's presence tonight had influenced her decision to invite Keith to the little get-together in the first place. While they spent time together outside of work, she'd never invited him to anything at her house without inviting others from Elite Force too. But Keith's comment at the airport after she accused him of having an aversion to any relationship that might lead somewhere had been occupying more of her thoughts than it should. And the devil in her wanted to see how he'd react when a woman let him know she was looking for some fun.

How he reacted shouldn't matter. Yet it did. Far more than she wished.

Across the way, Keith nodded and reached for his drink, successfully dislodging Jasmine's hand from his arm. In response, her friend leaned closer, and the sound of Maddie's teeth grinding together reminded her to relax her jaw before a trip to the dentist was in her immediate future.

Most of the men she worked with were handsome, perhaps not big-screen worthy, but they all earned themselves plenty of attention from the opposite sex. However, only one of them starred in her erotic dreams and had her waking up in the middle of the night wishing he was there so they could act out her fantasies. Keith. He made regular appearances in her fantasies, much to her annoyance, and had since day one.

Despite spending most of her adult life working in male-dominated fields, she'd never looked at a male coworker as any more than a friend, or in a few cases a person she avoided having any contact with outside of work. The first day Keith walked into the team meeting room, both her body and mind had sat up and taken notice. Perhaps not as handsome as Spike or Salty, something about the guy captured her attention and reminded her that although she did a job some might say should be carried out by men, she was a red-blooded woman.

In the beginning, she'd made sure to keep their relationship purely platonic, because they worked together and a romantic relationship in the workplace brought along a whole host of possible issues. As far as she was concerned, sex, no matter how good, wasn't worth risking her job over. Once she got to know him well and learned how much like her brother he was, she'd permanently nixed any possibility of them ever being anything more than friends. She didn't need the promise of a ring and a white picket fence, but she wanted a guy who could commit to her for more than forty-eight hours, something both Keith and her brother Spencer were incapable of doing. Spencer might not share specific details, but she heard about Keith's sex life regularly at work and knew he often spent time with a different woman every weekend. Definitely not the type of man she wanted to get involved with, no matter how many times she dreamed about him.

Or at least she'd thought so for the past year and a half. For reasons she couldn't explain, Keith's comment when he picked her up at the airport had her wondering if maybe she should reconsider her previous assessment.

Maddie's gaze moved away from Keith and Jasmine and toward Cassidy. Her friend had recently ended a two-year relationship with a man, and tonight she was letting Keith know she was available and very interested. Cassidy had spent most of the poker game practically sitting in Keith's lap. More than once, Maddie had caught him moving his chair in the opposite direction. Whether it was because Keith didn't want Cassidy to see his cards or because he wasn't interested in her was anyone's guess. Maddie wanted to believe it was because he wasn't interested, but a little voice kept reminding her this was Keith.

Much to her relief, Cassidy was no longer trying to crawl into his lap. When they finished playing cards, they brought all the appetizers and drinks outside. Now everyone was seated around the fire pit she'd had built after seeing the one at Salty's house earlier in the summer, and Cassidy hadn't snagged a seat next to him. Instead, Jasmine was on one side of him, and her next-door neighbor Declan was on the other.

"Are there any more buffalo wings inside?" Declan asked as he lifted the last one off the platter.

A recipe she'd spent months perfecting, she made buffalo wings for almost every gathering she hosted or attended, and they were always a hit.

"Yeah, I'll go heat more."

Declan licked the sauce from his fingers. The wings might be tasty, but they were also messy. "I can do it."

Maddie put down her can of soda and stood. "You're a guest. I don't mind. Does anyone else need anything?" She glanced around the group, and despite knowing better, her eyes lingered on Keith and Jasmine. At some point in the last few minutes, Jasmine had scooted her chair closer to his.

Spencer held up his empty bottle. A year older than Maddie, her brother had moved to the area earlier in the summer after accepting a position at Lafayette Laboratory and had been staying with her ever since. "Another hard cider if you remember."

She'd cooked the wings before everyone arrived, so she only needed to heat them tonight. After covering a tray with as many as would fit, she popped it in the oven and set the timer. Far too curious for her own good, she looked out the window. Whether Keith planned to accept the clear invitation Jasmine was sending him was none of her business. Still, her eyes zeroed in on the two of them. She couldn't be certain, but at least from here, it looked like he'd moved his chair away from the fire and to some extent Jasmine. Was it possible Keith wasn't interested in going back to Jasmine's place tonight?

Mind your own business. You're their friend, not their mother.

Annoyed at her inability to not care, she stalked across the kitchen and grabbed a hard cider from the refrigerator. After watching two of her friends throw themselves at Keith all night, she needed something stronger than root beer. Of course, neither of them knew how much their actions were bothering her. If they did, neither would ever make a move on him. But other than her sister, no one knew how she felt, and Maddie planned to keep it that way.

After taking a decent swig from the bottle, she leaned back against the counter and closed her eyes. Inviting Keith to see how he'd react to advances from her friends had been a colossal disaster, not to mention underhanded. The next time she got the notion to do something similar, she'd remind herself of tonight. Really, there wasn't anything worse than watching friends go after the man you wanted while knowing full well he might take them up on the offer.

"Hey, is everything okay?" Keith's sexy, velvety smooth voice alerted her to his presence. The man should be narrating romance novels or working at a radio station instead of working for Elite Force.

"Yeah. Just getting a little tired. Some coffee might help." Pushing off the counter, she set her drink down. "Do you want anything?"

"I came inside to see if you needed any help. But if you don't mind, I'll grab myself one of those." He pointed toward the hard cider on the counter.

"Help yourself." Maddie turned her attention to the cupboard where she usually kept the coffee filters. Most days she used the single-cup coffee machine that accepted the prefilled coffee pods. When she had guests, she opted for the traditional machine that let her brew an entire pot. Tonight, brewing enough for everyone gave her something to do besides focus on the man in the kitchen.

From the corner of her eye, she saw Keith reach for the bottle opener on the counter. His long, tan fingers closed around the handle, and a vision of them closing around her breasts formed.

Get your head back where it belongs. With more force than necessary, she pushed a can of soup out of the way in search of the elusive filters and a bag of coffee.

"Your brother reminds me of you. How long is Spencer staying here?"

Not finding the coffee or the filters on the first shelf, she moved her attention to the next one. "Spencer made an offer on a condo near Jasmine earlier this week, and the owners accepted it, so probably not too much longer."

Maddie pulled down the box of oatmeal, hoping to find the coffee filters hiding behind it. Once again she came up empty-handed. Where were the stupid things? Stretching, she moved a box of spaghetti on the third shelf out of the way.

Rather than take his drink and leave, Keith leaned against the counter and watched her. "Did Cassidy and Jasmine go with you to Myrtle Beach last weekend?"

Was this his way of getting more information on both women before he decided which one to go home with tonight?

"Only Cassidy did. She needed it. She just got out of a

long relationship and needed some time to vent." With the
spaghetti out of the way, she spotted the coffee. How it had
ended up so far back, she didn't know.

"You mean she needed a chance to man bash."

Yeah, they'd all done a little of that, but they hadn't spent
the entire weekend doing it. "Maybe a little." Grabbing the
coffee, she set it down next to the coffeepot and went back to
searching for the filters. "So which one is going to be the
lucky lady tonight? If you need help, I can distract one while
you leave with the other." She meant the statement to sound
like a joke but failed miserably.

"Thanks for the offer." He sounded hurt or perhaps
annoyed. Neither emotion made much sense.

After moving everything on the shelf and still not finding
what she wanted, Maddie gave up and opened another
cupboard.

"I know they're your friends, but part of the reason I
came in here was to get away from them both."

Her hand froze in the process of moving the cereal so she
could see what was behind it. He had two beautiful women
after him, and he wanted to get away from them? Coffee
filters forgotten, she turned. "Are you feeling okay? Should I
get the thermometer and check your temperature?"

Keith gave her a lazy grin and moved closer. She'd seen
him use it on women before, but she'd never had it directed at
her. Its effect was devastating. No wonder he never left a
bar alone.

"I'm feeling fine, but if you want to play nurse, I won't
stop you."

He's kidding around. Go along with it. "If you want a
nurse, we should call Neil. He was a medic in the navy."

Once again Keith stepped closer, but the grin he'd floored
her with a moment before was gone, replaced by a look she

couldn't fully label. It was an odd combination of seriousness and something bordering on uncertainty.

"I'm not interested in Neil either."

She felt his hands come down on her shoulders and watched as he lowered his head toward her. Yet somehow she couldn't move. Couldn't say anything to stop him.

Keith's lips brushed against hers. Whether she took the final step closer or he did, their bodies touched and the train engine in her chest kicked into a new gear.

As if they had a mind of their own, her arms went around his neck as he continued to move his lips gently against hers, never demanding anything but tenderly kissing her.

"Hey, Maddie, we're all out of salsa. Do we have any more?" Spencer's voice and the timer suddenly going off allowed her to do what she'd been unable to earlier, and she moved away.

Maddie nodded and then remembered Keith stood in front of her, making it difficult for her brother to see her. Clearing her throat, she headed for the oven. "There's a container in the refrigerator with more. Just take the whole thing outside." Like the buffalo wings, the salsa was a recipe she'd come up with.

Ignoring both the six-foot-two wall of muscle behind her and Spencer, she transferred the buffalo wings from the cookie sheet to a platter.

Keith had kissed her. What the hell should she take away from that? He'd told her he wasn't interested in Cassidy or Jasmine. Was it because he was eyeing her to be his weekend companion? Mentally she shook her head. Keith never had trouble finding someone to spend his time with. He wouldn't risk their working relationship for a night or two of sex. Maybe it had been an accident. Some kind of momentary brain fart where he'd forgotten how long they'd been friends.

The door into the backyard banged closed, signaling they were once again alone.

She didn't avoid difficult situations, no matter how no-win they seemed to be. She wasn't going to start now. Turning, she faced Keith. "You're not interested in the two women outside letting you know they'd be more than willing to leave with you tonight, and then you kiss me. What's going on with you, Keith?"

"If your brother hadn't interrupted us, I'd still be kissing you."

Spencer had either the worst or best timing. Either way, she wasn't going to let Keith get out of answering her question. "Keith?" The urge to plant her hands on her hips to let him know how serious she was nagged at her; unfortunately, she couldn't do it while holding a platter of wings.

Not that she had to worry about them for long. Keith advanced on her, reminding her of the tigers stalking their prey in the animal shows she used to watch. Without a word, he took the plate and set it down. "Ever since I walked inside the house, I've wanted to kiss you."

Keith, much like everyone else on the team, told it like it was. They didn't try to sugarcoat their words or leave you guessing their true meaning. She'd never been more grateful for that shared trait than now, because if Keith said he'd wanted to kiss her since he arrived, she knew he meant it.

Moving in closer, he touched her shoulder, his thumb slowly moving back and forth across her clavicle. "Do you have plans for tomorrow?"

He wasn't even touching her anyplace where it should matter, and yet her skin prickled with heat. What would happen if he ever put those hands and fingers elsewhere?

"No, not really." Laundry and vacuuming didn't constitute plans.

The same lazy grin that had nearly knocked Maddie on

her butt spread across his face. "Good. Let's do something together."

Before she could weigh the pros and cons and form a logical answer, he lowered his lips to hers again. Like before, he kept the kiss undemanding, but it didn't matter. It still caused her stomach to drop down to her toes.

"Whatever you want to do, we'll do," he added between passes across her lips.

A good idea or not, her brain could not form the word *no* while his lips were against hers. "Okay."

TEN

A soft, wet object nudged Kenzie in the shoulder a moment before nails scratched at the blankets near her hand. Opening her eyes, she pulled the blankets back so Marley could make his way underneath. Each night the dog fell asleep on top of the blankets down near her feet. However, at some point, he always woke up and decided he wanted to be under the blankets instead. To get Kenzie's attention, he always nudged her with his nose first. If Marley didn't get the outcome he wanted fast enough, he scratched the blankets. Usually, he made the request while the room was still dark, but that wasn't the case now. Maybe he'd had trouble falling asleep last night too, and once he had, he'd been too tired to move from his spot.

When she invited Ryan to stay the night, it'd been obvious he wanted to. It had actually taken him three tries before he successfully found his way back downstairs and to the front door. The first time he got out of bed, he pulled on his underwear before deciding a few more minutes together wouldn't hurt. The second time, he not only got his underwear on but his cargo shorts too. Once they managed to make

it all the way downstairs, it had still taken a little while before
he finally walked out the door. Despite the late hour, she'd
been wide awake, which wasn't a big surprise—sex always
woke her up better than an ice-cold shower. Knowing full
well it would be some time before she fell asleep, she tried
reading. She'd been trying to get through this sci-fi book for
weeks. Although not her usual type of novel—she preferred
mysteries, romances, and nonfiction books about history—
she'd tried it because her cousin couldn't stop raving about it.
So far, she didn't see what Megan liked about it. Last night
she'd trudged her way through chapter eight before tossing it
aside, probably for good this time. Still not tired, she'd made
herself a warm cup of milk—definitely not her favorite
beverage in the world unless it had a few heaping scoops of
cocoa powder mixed in, but it usually helped her fall asleep.
Last night had been no different, and when she climbed back
into bed, Marley had already been in his favorite spot snoring
away. She hadn't woken up once since then until now.

Reaching over, she grabbed her cell phone to check the
time. She wasn't in any rush to leave the comfort of her bed,
but she'd invited Ryan and his brother over for breakfast.
And unfortunately, she didn't have a magic wand that could
make a fully cooked meal appear, so she couldn't lounge
around in bed all morning, even if it sounded like an excellent
way to spend some time.

*A little before seven o'clock. Ten more minutes and I'll get
up.* Kenzie repositioned her pillow and let her mind wander to
her favorite subject these days. Even before Ryan had asked
her to join him and his friends a few weeks ago, she'd sensed
he was different than most of the men who'd passed through
her life. It wasn't so much the way he dressed or looked but
more the way he carried himself. He radiated confidence and
masculinity, reminding her of the knights in her favorite
medieval romance novels. At the same time, he didn't come

across as full of himself, an unfortunate symptom sometimes when individuals were confident in their abilities.

She'd been attracted to him long before he asked her out, partially because of those two traits. His friendly personality had also played a big role in her desire to get to know him better. And over the past couple of weeks, she'd gotten to know him better than she'd known her last boyfriend, and she'd dated Cullen for more than two months. The more Kenzie got to know Ryan, the more she liked him.

Okay, perhaps that wasn't a true statement. If she was being honest with herself, she was falling in love with him. Kenzie wasn't in the habit of ignoring the truth or lying to herself. She'd just never believed in love at first sight, or in this case love in less than a month. Relationships and affection took time.

She'd started dating her junior year of high school. Nothing serious, just the occasional date to the movies or the prom. It wasn't until the second semester of her freshman year of college that she got into a serious relationship with a man. Jordan had been a junior, and they probably wouldn't have met if he hadn't backed into her car in the library parking lot. Their relationship had started slowly, and months not weeks passed before she even suspected she loved him. Then around the time he got accepted to graduate school in Michigan, he asked her to marry him. She hadn't even needed to consider the question. She loved Jordan but didn't want to leave school in Virginia and relocate; not to mention, she didn't want to get married yet. He claimed he understood, and they agreed to try a long-distance relationship. After a few months, they both agreed it wasn't working. Oddly though, she hadn't been as heartbroken as she'd expected. Sure, she'd been sad. Jordan had been a big part of her life for two years, but she hadn't spent months moping around drowning her sorrow in junk food.

Since college, she'd had a few semiserious relationships, but she hadn't loved any of those men. Enjoyed spending time with them, sure. Liked and respected them, definitely. But she could honestly say she'd loved none of them.

Until now.

How could she not fall in love with Ryan? He'd spent a day walking around a botanical garden looking at flowers, an activity she knew he'd never do by himself, because she loved them. Then he cooked her dinner and bought her a birthday cake. Whenever they saw each other or talked on the phone, he asked about her day and listened when she answered. Perhaps the thing that sent her over the edge, though, was the fact he hadn't pressed her into having sex. He'd allow her to set the pace from day one. A lot of men she'd gone out with expected sex on the first date. Not surprisingly, those men never got a second one.

However, Ryan gave her complete control—well, at least until they landed in his bed yesterday. She'd had a few lovers, but he was in a league all his own.

Closing her eyes, she replayed the previous evening's activities. Somehow he'd known exactly where to touch her, making sure she enjoyed the experience just as much as him before even slipping inside her. And once he had, she'd been completely and utterly lost.

The sound of an old-fashioned telephone ringing filled the room, rudely interrupting the pleasant memories playing through Kenzie's head. She'd set the tone only for a handful of people, so she'd know in advance if the call was from someone important or not. So although she'd much prefer to keep daydreaming, she grabbed her cell phone. When she saw her cousin's name on the screen, it didn't surprise her. Megan often called on Saturdays, although usually the call came a little later in the day. Her cousin wasn't a morning person.

"I hope I didn't wake you," Megan said.

Kenzie moved into an upright position, the movement earning her a disgruntled look from Marley. "Nah, I was about to get out of bed anyway. Ryan and his brother are coming over for breakfast." Beloved cousin or not, Megan didn't need to know she'd been thinking about all the ways Ryan had pleasured her the night before and how she hoped he would tonight.

"He has a brother."

"Three, actually." Kenzie smiled, already knowing what Megan's reaction would be when she announced Ryan and Adam were identical twins. "Adam, the one coming this morning, is Ryan's twin."

"Your next-door neighbor has a twin. Are they identical?"

"So much so I almost kissed the wrong one yesterday."

"Oh my God. You didn't. Was Ryan mad?"

"No, until yesterday I didn't know he and Adam were identical."

"Are they the same in every way?" Megan asked.

Kenzie knew her cousin wasn't referring to their personalities. While she hadn't intentionally examined Adam's physique, it looked darn close to Ryan's. "Let's just say your Mr. Too-Yummy-For-Words nickname applies to Adam too."

"Once I get back home, I might have to plan a trip down to see you."

"Still in Bristol?" If her cousin was still in England, which was five hours ahead of Virginia, it explained why she'd called early again.

"I leave on Friday."

Kenzie scratched Marley behind his ear, and in return, he licked her wrist. "You're welcome to visit, but Adam won't be around. At least I don't think he will. He lives in North Carolina. He stopped to visit on his way to see his parents in New Hampshire."

"Hmm, well, if he plans on stopping by again when he

heads back home, let me know and I might conveniently find myself sleeping in your spare bedroom."

Rolling her eyes, Kenzie grabbed her wristwatch and checked the time. As much as she'd love to sit and chat, she needed to get her butt in gear. "Will do." Megan liked to talk big, but when it came to men, she was rather shy, so even if Adam and Megan ever found themselves in each other's company, she wouldn't make a move on him. "Unfortunately, right now I need to get going."

After she prepared a cup of tea, Kenzie did a quick inventory of the ingredients she had on hand. She could easily whip up some pancakes and scrambled eggs, but both were boring. If she'd known in advance that she would be cooking breakfast this morning, yesterday she would've picked up everything she needed to make corn beef hash and roasted potatoes. Unfortunately, the idea to invite Ryan over this morning had only come to her as they were lying in bed last night.

German pancakes weren't as ordinary as traditional pancakes, and she hadn't had them in months. Plus, she had all the ingredients on hand. While she was at it, she'd make them all southwestern omelets. Again, not as boring as plain scrambled eggs, and the refrigerator contained everything she needed.

Ryan checked his watch. Kenzie told him to come over around eight thirty. It was already ten past eight and his brother had yet to make an appearance. At another time, he'd give Adam a pass. After he'd returned from Kenzie's house, they'd sat around the fire pit talking and drinking beer for a couple of hours. Honestly, he'd love a few more hours of sleep this morning. With that impossible, he was relying on caffeine to give him the boost he needed.

"Nice of you to finally join me," Ryan greeted when Adam strolled in the kitchen, his hair still damp from a shower.

His brother walked past him without even looking in his direction and grabbed a coffee cup from the cupboard. "Good morning to you too. I'll be sure to let Kenzie know how rude you were to me." Adam took his time selecting a coffee pod and then setting it inside the single-serve coffee maker with all the precision of a surgeon. "Do you want another?"

"I'll get it myself." Ryan wasn't going to give his brother any excuse to intentionally drag his feet, and that was exactly what he was doing. They had their differences, but when it came to being on time, it was a trait they shared. Today Adam was taking his sweet time and risking the possibility they might be late just to annoy him.

Adam shrugged as he sat on one of the stools around the island. Then while Ryan watched, he added cream and carefully measured out sugar as if he was making a cake rather than a cup of coffee. Once finished, he mixed the contents, removed the spoon, and set it on a napkin. His brother was going all out this morning in his efforts to get on his nerves.

After downing the last of his coffee, Ryan walked to the counter for another. Two, even oversized ones like he'd just finished, would not cut it this morning. "Are you going to drink it or look at it?"

"It needs to cool. I don't want to burn my tongue and then not be able to enjoy breakfast."

Yeah, he'd remember this and be sure to repay the favor at a later date.

Adam blew across the top of the cup, something Ryan hadn't seen his brother do since they were ten years old and they made hot chocolate after playing in the snow all day.

"Last time you were this excited about breakfast was when we got to eat with our favorite characters down in Florida."

He remembered the trip. It'd been the first time their parents took them to the theme parks in Orlando. On their second morning there, they'd eaten breakfast while their favorite characters strolled through the restaurant posing for pictures and autographs. Yeah, he had been excited for that particular meal, so much so he'd barely slept the night before. What he was feeling now wasn't excitement. It was more anticipation. Once he left his house, he had a whole day and night with Kenzie to look forward to. And since Adam wouldn't be around tonight, if Kenzie invited him to spend the night again, he'd take her up on the offer.

Finally, Adam sipped his coffee. "Perfect."

"What a relief." Ryan took a swig from his cup.

The raised coffee cup didn't hide Adam's grin. "Don't worry, we won't be late. I like Kenzie, and I wouldn't want to do anything that'll earn me a black mark in her book, just in case she realizes she could do much better with me."

"In your dreams."

Despite his brother's theatrics, Ryan rang Kenzie's doorbell at exactly eight thirty. Right on cue, Marley's dulcet tones reached them outside.

"Great timing." Kenzie didn't hesitate as she reached for his hand.

He'd wondered if she'd be able to tell them apart this morning. It usually took people a while before they could tell them apart, and she'd only met Adam yesterday. In fact, except for their friends in school, many of their classmates had always looked at their shoes or their backpacks to help identify them. Today, nothing about their outfits would help Kenzie. Since they had similar taste in clothes, they were both dressed in cargo shorts and plain T-shirts, his being dark blue while Adam's was gray. Even their shoes were a similar style.

"The pancakes need about another two minutes in the oven," Kenzie said.

He'd been eating pancakes all his life, and he'd never heard of anyone making them in the oven. But hey, there was a first for everything.

If it was her father standing there, he'd think twice, but it wasn't. Reaching for Kenzie's waist, he pulled her close. As if they'd been doing it all their lives, her arms went around his neck as he lowered his mouth to hers. The taste and feel of her lips against his did what three cups of coffee hadn't been able to. The sluggish fog in his head cleared, and energy pulsed through his body. Ryan moved a hand and cradled her head while he traced the seam of her lips, urging her to open for him.

Denied his usual greeting, Marley nudged the back of his leg, but he ignored it. He'd give the dog some attention after. Maybe even a treat or two, if he behaved later tonight and didn't bother them too much.

"I think that's our cue to beat it, buddy," Adam said, and the nudging against Ryan's leg stopped.

Later he'd have to thank his brother.

When he finally came up for air, she smiled at him, nearly knocking him on his ass. How rude would it be to leave his brother to eat alone while they went upstairs?

"I think I hear the timer." Moving out of his embrace, she took his hand again. "I hope you're hungry."

As if to answer, his stomach rumbled.

Fresh fruit and toast were already on the kitchen table. Three covered pans sat on the stove, and the barest hint of something sweet filled the air.

"Kenzie, your dog and I were just about to help ourselves to whatever you have on the stove. It's a good thing you got here when you did," Adam said as he scratched Marley, who sat at his feet.

After she shut off the timer, she pulled open the oven door. "He knows better. Well, at least most of the time."

Ryan couldn't stop himself from watching as she bent over to pull the oven rack out. This morning she had on a pair of denim shorts that encased the sexiest ass he'd ever seen, and much later he fully planned to help her out of them. She'd paired them with a Washington National's T-shirt, an appropriate choice considering their destination this afternoon.

"You can't say the same about my brother," Ryan said as he dragged his eyes away from the oven and glanced at his brother. Like a good boy, Adam's attention was still on Marley, not the enticing image at the stove.

She set a small cast-iron skillet on the stove before reaching into the oven for another. "Help yourself to what's on the table or coffee. The cups are in the cabinet near the dishwasher."

Adam didn't waste any time getting up. "Do either of you want some?"

Ryan nodded, his eyes once again following Kenzie as she worked.

"My cup is on the counter," she called over her shoulder.

"I've never heard of anyone making pancakes in the oven. Is it some kind of family recipe or something you came up with?" Kenzie had told him she liked to experiment in the kitchen.

"You've never had German pancakes?" Carefully she removed one golden brown pancake from the pan and placed it on a plate. "Sometimes they're called bismarcks."

Shaking his head, Ryan accepted the coffee his brother handed him. "Not that I remember. I have had French toast."

Kenzie uncovered one of the pans on the stove and added

the omelet inside to the plate. "Much like with French toast, these pancakes have no ties to the country they are named after."

He'd always assumed French toast, at least the way it was made in the United States, wasn't a traditional French food, but he'd never cared enough to find out for sure. Still, it was nice to know he'd been right.

She repeated the process at the stove and carried two plates over. "I prefer fruit on mine, but maple syrup tastes good on them too. Sometimes I'll use both."

Slices of avocado and salsa covered the omelets, and Ryan added both strawberries and maple syrup to his pancake before digging in.

"How long are you staying in New Hampshire?" Kenzie dropped into the seat next to him, her plate identical to his and Adam's.

Knowing his brother, it wouldn't be a long visit. The guy never took more than a week off from work. While his job required a lot of hours, Adam went above and beyond. He was a textbook example of a workaholic, a trait Ryan was glad he hadn't inherited from their mom. Actually, of the six Saltarelli children, only Adam and Vanessa seemed to share the trait with their mom.

Washing down a mouthful of food with coffee, he shrugged. "Four or five days. I plan to stop and visit a friend in Rhode Island for a day or so before I head home."

Ryan admired his brother's work ethic and dedication, but the guy needed to live a little. Now wasn't the time or place to again give Adam advice.

"I've spent time in New England, but I've never visited Rhode Island," Kenzie commented as she covered her pancake with berries and then maple syrup.

"There are some nice beaches in Newport and Narragansett. Not as nice as the one in Virginia Beach, but I always preferred them to the ones in Maine and New Hampshire. You can get some pretty good seafood in Rhode Island too."

He had to disagree with his brother there. He much preferred the beaches in New Hampshire. The ones in Narragansett and especially those in Newport were too crowded.

"My parents have a house in Virginia Beach. I love it down there. I wish I had more time to visit when they're there." With the top of her pancake completely hidden under a layer of fresh fruit, Kenzie reached for a fork and a knife. "When you drive home, are you going to stop and spend the night again?"

Unless in a rush, Adam always made a pit stop both on his way north and then on the return trip.

Adam smiled, a forkful of omelet almost to his mouth. "Hoping for another chance to compare us and make sure you picked the right brother?"

Under the table, Kenzie squeezed Ryan's thigh. "Believe me, after last night, I *know* I'm with the right one. I was just curious."

His brother pulled out the sad, heartbroken expression he'd perfected when they were kids. "Hey, I understand. But if he ever treats you poorly, call me and I'll take care of him for you." Adam cut into his pancake, but again it didn't reach its final destination because he was too busy talking. "Depending on when I leave Rhode Island, I might just drive straight home."

"Well, I have a cousin I think would be perfect for you. If I can convince her to visit me soon, maybe you could plan another trip this way."

ELEVEN

Anywhere within a ten-mile radius of Protection First was the last place Gabe should be. Ever since he'd gotten the information from Sam listing where Armstrong and his wife lived and worked, he'd been battling with himself. Keeping his distance and allowing Zane's boys to follow the couple and report back to him with their daily routines was the safe move. He didn't want anything to tip Armstrong off. But despite days of surveillance, late yesterday afternoon had been the first time Jax had seen the couple enter their house.

When he got the text saying Armstrong and his wife were home, he'd lost the battle he'd been winning until then. After kicking his last client's ass in the ring, he jumped on Interstate 95 and headed north. He'd spent the night at one of the chain hotels in the area.

Despite the fairly comfortable bed and the bottle of scotch he'd picked up while getting takeout, rather than sleep, he'd sat on the balcony and considered his options for today, only going inside when the sun appeared in the sky. He could park on Armstrong's street and watch the house for any sign of the guy or his wife. If he did, he risked some nosey neighbors noticing him and calling the cops. He'd gone above and beyond to avoid any run-ins with the cops since his release from prison. These days he even followed the speed limit to avoid getting pulled over. So although he was more likely to see the guy at his house, watching Armstrong's business was a safer bet.

Gabe accepted the frozen-fruit concoction and the sandwich from the employee behind the counter and then returned to the table he'd been camped at most of the day, pretending to work on his laptop. Located at the front of the café, it provided him with a front-row view of Protection First across the street. It also let him see anyone approaching the café's entrance before they walked inside, because the last thing he needed was Edward Armstrong strolling in for lunch and seeing him. When they came face-to-face again, it would be on Gabe's terms.

A group of college-aged women dressed in workout clothes exited the self-defense and firearms school. With nothing better to do, he'd checked the schedule on the company's website to see if Armstrong was teaching today. While the website listed the names of the classes, the times, and a brief description of each one, there was no instructor's name included. En masse, the group crossed the street and headed for the café door.

According to the website, the school closed at four o'clock on Saturdays, and that was three hours away. He'd already been sitting inside the café since eight. As long as he continued to make purchases, management had no reason to ask him to leave, but he wasn't sure he'd manage another hour in here, never mind three. The beverages and food tasted great, but overpriced cafés that used names he could barely pronounce for their beverages sizes while playing French music were not the type of places he spent his time. And the music was French. He remembered just enough from the four years he'd taken in high school to recognize many of the words.

No, these days he preferred bars that served beer and burgers. A place where he could play a game of pool or find a woman interested in nothing but some sex. There had been a period in his life when he'd stopped visiting those type of places. Instead, he'd spent his nights and weekends with Savannah, Logan, and Ava. Thanks to Armstrong, those days no longer existed. Now his ex-wife lived in Denver, closer to her family, and he hadn't seen or spoken to his children since the day the FBI arrested him.

Bored out of his mind, Gabe allowed memories of the weekends with his family to emerge from the locked box he kept them in, thoughts he rarely let out because of the black place they always brought him to.

"Maybe you should offer to buy him lunch after class next week," one of the women who'd left Protection First and come inside the café said as she joined her friends at a table near his.

"He's old enough to be her father, Caitlyn," a second woman with long blonde hair streaked with pink added, pulling out another chair at their table.

"I didn't say I wanted to go out with him. Only that I think he's handsome, in an older-man, silver-fox sort of way," her friend replied. "I wonder if he has a son? If he does, I bet he's gorgeous."

A fourth woman placed a frozen drink on the table and pulled out a chair. "Someone in class told me he has a daughter. I don't know if they're right."

"Why don't you ask him, Lisa? I think he's coming in here."

The blonde's comment had Gabe glancing toward the windows just in time to see Edward Armstrong crossing the street. Rage started in his belly and streaked out in every direction, pushing everything from his mind, and his vision clouded.

He could take him out here. Although not sharp, the butter knife he'd gotten with his sandwich would do the job if inserted in the right place.

He won't suffer that way. Gabe released the knife he hadn't even realized he'd picked up until then. Angling his chair away from the door, he focused on his keyboard. At the table next to him, the four women called out greetings to Armstrong, and Gabe mentally swore. All he needed was the guy to stop and start up a conversation with the women.

The guy didn't linger. After he returned their greetings, the women's conversation turned to their plans for the evening, and Gabe tuned them out.

When he'd sat down, he turned off the sound on his cell phone, not because he cared about disturbing anyone else but because he didn't want to call attention to himself. Now the device on the table vibrated, and he saw Sam Nixon's number on the screen. He didn't want to let the call go to voice mail. He'd been waiting to hear from the guy since their last meeting. If Armstrong was close enough to hear his voice, what were the odds he'd hear it over the other conversations going on inside the café or even recognize it?

Slim. And things were taking longer than he liked already. Gabe couldn't miss this call and add in more delays.

"Yeah," he greeted.

"I have the information you wanted."

He didn't bother asking for any details. Sam wouldn't give him any more until he got paid.

"Do you want to meet me at my office again or should I come to the gym?" Sam asked.

Fuck. Both the gym and Sam's office were three-plus hours away. Not that he wanted to meet the private investigator at either, but Sam's office was the better option. Saturdays, the gym was either packed or dead. There was no way to know which it would be tonight. Not to mention, his brother might be there. Xander didn't spend much time at the gym on the weekends, but occasionally if his kids had other plans, he'd spend a few hours catching up on work. If Xander saw him meeting with Sam, he'd ask who Sam was, and Gabe would have to lie.

"I'll meet you at your office, but I'm not in the area right now. Around six work for you?" On paper, the drive took three hours and forty minutes. In reality, thanks to traffic, it always took longer, and he'd need to stop home and get the guy's money.

"Yeah, see you then."

Unlike on Gabe's first visit, the door separating the waiting area from the rest of the space was open tonight, and he took that as an invitation to make his way down to Sam's office.

Looking up, Sam gestured for Gabe to enter the room. "If anything changes, call me," he said to whoever was on the other end of the line.

He hadn't driven all the way to listen to Sam's conversation.

"Otherwise I'll talk to you tomorrow night," Sam continued before ending the call and dropping the cell phone on his desk next to a flash drive.

He knew the routine, so he didn't wait for Sam to ask for it. Opening his gym bag, he removed the envelope and handed it over. "Payment first. I know."

After counting the money, Sam unlocked a desk drawer and deposited it inside. "Your old friend has one daughter." Sam slid the flash drive toward him as he relocked the drawer. "Her name is Kenzie Armstrong, and she lives in

Dumfries and works at Parkview, an immediate care clinic about thirty minutes from her house."

"Does she live alone?" If he decided they should take her from the house, it'd be easier if she lived alone.

"As far as I can tell. It's only her name on the mortgage, and the day I followed her I didn't see anyone else at the house."

Gabe would verify that before he made any final plans. He didn't want a boyfriend or a roommate making a sudden appearance and complicating things.

"Everything I uncovered about her is on the drive, including some photos of her."

The information in his palm took him another step closer.

"Is there anything else you need?"

Most people were creatures of habit. They left their house around the same time. Took the same route to work every day. Visited the same stores and restaurants. His next step was to learn these things about Kenzie Armstrong. He didn't need the private investigator for that. Like he was doing with Armstrong and his wife, he'd use guys he trusted.

"I have everything I need. Thanks."

Gabe didn't stick around and bullshit with the guy. With the flash drive safely in his pocket, he climbed back in his car, more eager than he'd been in a long time to get home.

TWELVE

Without opening her eyes, Kenzie rolled over and threw out an arm, expecting it to land on either the cotton sheet or her dog. Instead, it landed on something much larger and smoother. It took her brain a moment to register that her arm was on top of Ryan's chest.

After the baseball game yesterday, they'd stopped at a farmers' market they passed on their way home. There had been vendors there selling everything from freshly picked tomatoes to locally raised beef, homemade ice cream, and gorgeous plants. They'd taken their time strolling around before selecting some steaks, a variety of veggies, and some homemade ice cream that had looked too good to pass up. She'd even picked up a few new perennials for her yard because they'd been too pretty to not buy. Back at her house, Ryan offered to grill the steaks while she prepared whatever she wanted to go with them. She'd turned him down. Actually, he'd seemed a little put out when she insisted on doing the cooking herself, but in her house, she did the grilling—unless her dad was around, and then occasionally she'd hand over her apron and spatula, but she only did so grudgingly because her dad considered himself the king of the grill, a well-earned title.

Once they could both stand the sight of food again, they indulged in ice cream sundaes while relaxing outside and talking until a soft drizzle sent them in the house. Even before the rain forced them back inside though, she asked him to spend the night. Unlike the previous evening, he didn't decline the invitation, a fact Marley hadn't been too happy about, because once she'd let him in the bedroom, she'd forced him to sleep on the dog bed she kept in the room even though he never used it.

Kenzie opened her eyes and found Ryan on his back, one arm tucked under his head and his eyes on her. "How long have you been awake?" She snuggled in closer to him.

"About an hour."

"You could've woken me up." She'd go crazy just hanging around in bed for that long without at least a book to read or the television on.

She felt his shoulder move as he shrugged. "I didn't want to. You looked peaceful." Shifting onto his side, he kissed her forehead and wrapped an arm around her. "I can't say the same about your dog. I think he's planning ways to kill me. You should see the looks he gives me every time he comes over."

"It's probably a good idea to watch your back. You are in Marley's spot. Maybe you should hire one of your friends from work to protect you."

"He sleeps in your bed every night? Lucky dog."

She opened her mouth, ready to tell him he was more than welcome to sleep in her bed every night. Before the words escaped, she caught herself. Men could be weird. He might interpret the comment to mean she wanted them to move in together, which she didn't. If he assumed that was what she meant, he might decide he wasn't ready for that kind of commitment and bolt out the door. At the same time, he might reach the same conclusion and decide they should live together, a step she wasn't ready to make yet.

As if he knew they were talking about him, Marley jumped onto the bed, settled his head on her leg, and stared at them as if trying to control their minds. The next time Ryan spent the night, she'd have to reconsider letting Marley in the room at all. He could just as easily sleep on the bed in the spare room or downstairs on the sofa.

Where the dog spent the night was a problem for another day. For the moment, he could hang out at the foot of the bed.

"What do you want to do today?" Since he seemed to be in no rush to leave, she guessed he didn't have any plans today, and she had nothing on her calendar either.

Gently he worked free the hair tie holding her loose ponytail in place. Then he dragged his fingers through her hair. She'd noticed he often pulled her hair free whenever she wore it up. "Whatever you want."

The fingers in her hair moved, and Ryan started to massage the back of her neck. The baseball game yesterday was his idea, but they'd gone because she was a Nationals fan, not him. She didn't have as much relationship experience as her parents or grandparents, but she knew that to be successful, a relationship couldn't be one-sided.

"There's nothing specific I feel like doing. But I'm open to some suggestions." Of course, if he wanted to stay in bed all day and massage her back, she wouldn't object either. Somehow he was finding knots she hadn't even realized she had in her neck.

"Spike is having a cookout at his house. He invited us. I wasn't sure you were ready for another round with my friends." The fingers massaging her neck slipped lower and started working on her shoulder instead. Once again he located and worked out a knot she'd not noticed until now.

She'd enjoyed herself the last time she'd been around his friends. Kenzie didn't see why this time would be any different. "Do you think he'll be willing to share some embarrassing stories about you?"

Spike and Ryan had grown up together. Other than his siblings, there wasn't anyone in the world more qualified to provide her with some interesting stories. At least it was true when it came to her cousin Megan. Her cousin could probably fill an entire book with the embarrassing things she'd done over the years. Of course, Kenzie had a decent number of stories she could share about Megan too. Before Ryan and Megan ever came to face-to-face, she'd have to have a sit-down with her cousin and spell out exactly which stories she could under no circumstances ever share.

"You won't even have to ask him."

Unlike the previous morning when she'd cooked for Ryan and his brother, they worked together in the kitchen preparing breakfast, making the task far more enjoyable. However, it also meant it took twice as long as it should have to prepare pancakes, omelets, and bacon. Somehow though, even with the distractions, she only burned two pancakes—ones Marley happily ate with a dab of maple syrup. The bacon was another story. After successfully mixing up some pancake batter, she added several slices of bacon to the skillet on the stove while Ryan worked on chopping up fresh veggies for their omelets. Or at least that was what he was supposed to be doing. Instead, he took a break from chopping peppers, wrapped his arms around her waist, and kissed her neck, starting just below her ear and making his way down to her shoulder. As if that wasn't distracting enough, he moved his hands up and gently massaged her breasts until she finally turned and kissed him. Okay, maybe she'd done a little more than simply kiss him. She'd used her mouth and hands to express the words she suspected were true but wasn't ready to share yet.

At least until the smoke alarm went off, alerting them to the fact the bacon had gone from something they could eat to something only fit for the trash. Thankfully, her second attempt at cooking the breakfast meat went as planned, as did the omelets Ryan prepared.

After adding the final dirty plate, Kenzie closed the dishwasher and hit Start. "Should we bring anything to Spike's house?" She realized it was an outdated custom, but her mom always insisted on bringing something when she went to someone's house for dinner or a cookout. Unless a person specifically told her not to, Kenzie did the same.

"I didn't ask, and he didn't say. It's up to you."

"Let's stop at Sugar and Spice on the way." She didn't know where Spike lived, but regardless of where it was, the bakery was less than ten minutes from them, so it shouldn't add too much time to their drive.

Ryan's lips parted, but rather than speak, he snapped them shut and nodded. "Sounds good. Everything they make is great." Stepping closer, he wrapped his arms around her and lowered his mouth toward hers. "It won't take me long to shower. Come on over whenever you're ready."

Or you can bring your stuff here and we can shower together. An image of Ryan naked in her shower washing her back passed through her head, and a wave of heat washed over her. It made little sense for him to walk home, grab his stuff, and come back. The next time he spent the night though, she'd suggest he bring everything he needed for the following day so they could help each other get ready.

His lips touched hers, but they didn't linger, and considering the images and thoughts going through her head, it was probably a good thing if they hoped to leave her house today.

"I'll be over soon," she promised.

Releasing her, he stepped back and shrugged. "Don't rush. There's no set start time for the cookout. Spike has a heated pool, so you might want to bring a bathing suit." Ryan gave Marley a quick scratch behind his ears. "See you later, Marley."

As if he understood Ryan was leaving, the dog licked Ryan's hand and then started walking toward the front door.

"I think he's telling me it's time to go."

"Well, you did take his spot in bed last night. It might be a little while before he forgives you." Kenzie smiled and walked with him to the door where Marley was waiting. Since the dog always used the door in the kitchen when he wanted to go out, she knew he wasn't waiting there because he needed to relieve himself. "Maybe if you bring over some treats next time, you'll be back in his good graces again."

Standing on the step and watching Ryan walk back to his house wasn't the best use of her time, but it was without a doubt enjoyable. The man really had an incredible ass. Well, in her opinion, he had an incredible everything, but this particular angle allowed her to focus on that sexy attribute.

Showered and dressed, Ryan sent Spike a text message telling him they'd be over and asking if he needed anything—not that he expected his friend did. But if Spike came back and said he needed more burgers or some potato chips, it'd be a good excuse to skip going to Sugar and Spice, because it was in the opposite direction of the supermarket.

Spike wouldn't care if they showed up empty-handed, and if he wanted you to bring something, he'd let you know ahead of time. However, he understood why Kenzie wanted to arrive with food in hand. Whenever his mom went to someone's house, regardless of whether it was the first time or the fortieth time, she brought something along. Most of the time, it was a pie or some other dessert she baked, but occasionally she'd bring along a nice bottle of wine. If they were going to a cookout thrown by one of Kenzie's friends, he'd want to bring something along too, so he didn't mind stopping on their way to Spike's. He just didn't want to stop at that bakery. While they made some of the best pastries and desserts in the area, he didn't want to risk running into Ariana, the bakery's co-owner, today.

They'd met one night at Shooter's, a nearby pub he frequently stopped at on his way home and on the weekends. After a few drinks and two rounds of pool, she'd invited him back to her house. To say they'd had a relationship would be a stretch. They'd been more what Mad Dog referred to as sex buddies, an arrangement that had worked for both of them. He hadn't heard from her in roughly three months. Whether or not that was because she was with someone, he didn't know and didn't care. He had no interest in their previous arrangement. If she was working today, Ryan didn't think she'd say anything to him with Kenzie standing there, but he'd rather not find out either. And if she did, Kenzie might just shrug it off. Or she might not. He wasn't sure how he'd react if they ran into one of her former lovers.

No, that was a lie. Ryan would want to make sure the guy knew he'd blown it and that Kenzie was no longer available. Not only was she not single, but she wouldn't be again if he had anything to say about it.

He'd known their relationship was different, but until last night, he hadn't realized just how deep he was in already.

Ryan's phone chimed, and the doorbell rang at the same time. The text confirmed what he'd assumed. Spike had everything he needed, and they could stop by whenever they wanted. Shoving the phone back in his pocket, he opened the door. "That didn't take you long."

"I perfected the art of a quick shower a long time ago. I'm ready to go if you are."

Two college friends owned Sugar and Spice, which was

located in a large shopping plaza along with a butcher, dance school, hair salon, and a pizza joint. According to the sign out front, the place had been in business for five years, and thanks to his involvement with Ariana, he knew the two friends planned to expand the business by taking over the empty store next door to the bakery.

Ryan pulled his Mustang into a spot in front of the butcher. It was too nice of a day to leave the convertible in the garage, especially since in another few months he wouldn't want to take the car on the road.

"Looks like they're making the bakery bigger." Kenzie pointed toward the empty storefront between Sugar and Spice and the butcher. The last time he'd been in the plaza, a For Lease sign had filled the store window. Now the name of the bakery was on the glass. "Business must be good." Without waiting for him, she got out of the car.

Catching up with her on the sidewalk, he put his arm around her shoulders. If Ariana was working today, he wanted her to see them come in together. "The few times I've stopped in, there have always been people here."

"I'm not surprised. Everything I've bought here has been delicious. And the custom cakes they make look amazing. Did you see the picture of the guitar cake they made hanging up on the wall?"

He'd noticed the various pictures hanging on the walls inside, but he'd never bothered to examine any of them. "I don't think so."

When they entered, he could just make out the music playing inside. Although he'd heard the song before, he couldn't put a name to it or identify the artist singing. He did know where he'd heard it before though: at Ariana's house. She liked to have music on during sex.

While they waited for their turn, he studied the chalk-boards hanging on the wall. In addition to making traditional cupcakes, brownies, and mini cakes, the bakery featured special flavors each week. The boards also listed the various types of pies and French macaroons available today.

"Rocky road brownies sound good. Maybe we should get a few of those and half a dozen peanut buttercream cupcakes and half a dozen chocolate hazelnut cupcakes."

"And a fresh blueberry pie." Nothing reminded him of summer like a fresh blueberry pie, especially if made with wild Maine blueberries. Ryan moved so he could hold open the door for a woman holding an enormous cake box. When he came back inside, he found Ariana smiling at him as she came around the display case.

"Hey, Ryan." She didn't hesitate to give him a kiss and a hug. "It's been a while. How are you?"

Kenzie didn't react to the greeting, but her eyes darted in Ariana's direction before settling on him again. He could almost see the gears in her head working as she came up with ways they might know each other.

Before answering, he draped his arm over Kenzie's shoulders again and pulled her in close. "Good. You?" Limiting their conversation seemed the best course of action, but he tried never to be rude either.

"Busy, but good. When I have more time, we should catch up."

Hell no. "Kenzie and I are heading up to New Hampshire soon. If you have some free time when we get back, maybe we can all get together?"

Understanding passed across her eyes, and she smiled. "Sure. I'll call you. What can I get for you today?"

Later he'd have some explaining to do, but his statement had gotten his point across. Ariana knew he was with someone and wouldn't be calling him despite what she'd said.

Kenzie didn't speak again until they were in the car and

he was backing out of the parking space. "My invitation must have gotten lost. I didn't know we were going to New Hampshire soon, or was that some kind of message to who I'm guessing is an ex-girlfriend?"

He could let Kenzie think he'd been in a romantic relationship with the bakery owner. If he did, though, later he'd feel guilty about lying to her. "I wouldn't call her an ex, but we've spent time together. Today is the first time I've seen her in months." Shifting the car into first gear, Ryan headed for the exit and waited for Kenzie's response. One he wasn't sure he wanted to hear, but it was better to get everything out in the open now.

"Gotcha." Judging by her tone, she knew exactly how they'd spent their time together. Oddly, she didn't sound upset. "And telling her we're going away soon was your way of letting her know not to expect any calls from you in the near future." Kenzie moved in her seat, allowing her to see him better.

More like ever. "You could say that. But I did plan to ask if you'd go up with me for Thanksgiving." Turning out of the parking lot, he shifted gears again. "If you can't make it, I was going to suggest we go up for a weekend before then."

"Thanksgiving is a few months away. I wouldn't exactly call that soon. But sure, I'll go with you. My parents always head to my grandmother's house for the holiday. There are always so many people there, no one will even realize I'm missing. If you want to go up sooner though, I'm up for a little getaway. Give me a date, and I'll make sure I have the weekend off."

Unlike the cookie-cutter neighborhood they lived in, Spike's house was one of only four on the street. Except for Spike's, they'd all been constructed within the past decade, and judging by the swing sets and basketball nets at the other homes, they were all occupied by families.

With no room left in the driveway, Ryan parked on the street behind Connor's truck and put the car's top up. He didn't want to come out and find the seats covered in bird shit.

"Did you ever see the movie *Anne of Green Gables*?" Kenzie gazed at Spike's house as she accepted the pie he held out.

In fourth grade, he had no other choice but to read the book after he waited too long to get a historical fiction book from the library for a book report. With only two days left of winter break, he grabbed one from his older sister's bookshelf. At the time she only had two possibilities: *Anne of Green Gables* and *Little Women*. He'd gone with the one that looked shorter. After that, he'd never procrastinated again when a teacher assigned a book report.

"Nope."

"This house reminds me of the one in the movie, only bigger."

He'd take her word on it. "The place was in rough shape when Spike bought it. He salvaged as much of the original structure as he could and then put on an addition, expanding the kitchen. The garage is the old carriage house. There was no saving the barn."

"My parents remodeled their kitchen after they bought their house in Virginia Beach, and it cost a pretty penny. I don't even want to know what the work on this place must have cost."

He didn't know the final dollar amount, but it would have been much cheaper if Spike had had a new house similar to his own built. Not that it mattered, since his friend could afford it. Spike's great-grandfather had made his fortune with coal mines—mines his grandfather and uncle still ran. Although Spike's dad had nothing to do with the company, as one of the top neurosurgeons in Boston, he wasn't lacking for funds either.

"Spike's got a thing for old houses. Two years ago, he bought an old log cabin up near Lake Winnipesaukee. He stays there in the winter when he goes skiing. About once a year, I'll go with him."

"He can keep his old houses. I enjoy looking at them, especially those from the Victorian era, but I'd never want to live in one. Mom grew up in one so old a section of the basement floor is dirt. My grandparents still live there. Nana has lost count of how many mice and bats she's come across while down there doing laundry. To this day, I hate going in their basement."

Ryan bypassed the front door and followed the voices and music to the backyard. "Mice and bats don't bother me, but I wouldn't want to share my house with either."

Several members of HRT, including Ax, their boss, were already in the yard. There were also a handful of people who worked in Elite Force's cyber division—or perhaps he should call them magicians. He didn't know how they did what they did, but when it came to computers and getting information, nothing stopped them.

"Glad you two made it." Spike clapped him on the shoulder and then added more beer to the cooler near the table. Then he turned his attention toward Kenzie. "It's nice to see you again. Help yourself to whatever you want. The burgers and sausages are on the grill now, and Mad Dog is heating the buffalo wings she brought."

"Any specific place you want the desserts?" Kenzie asked. At the moment the table closest to them was overflowing with typical cookout foods, and there was no way the bakery boxes would fit.

Spike glanced at the boxes they each held. "You stopped at Sugar and Spice. Nice. Everything they make tastes great."

Ryan saw the unasked question in his friend's eyes. Spike knew about his and Ariana's relationship, and he was wondering if Ryan had run into the bakery's co-owner. Ryan nodded slightly. "Thank Kenzie, it was her idea."

"Why don't you put them inside for now," Spike said.

Mad Dog was transferring her homemade buffalo wings from the baking sheet to a large platter, and although on the phone, Keith stood less than a foot from her at the counter.

"Finally, a reinforcement," Mad Dog said, coming toward them. "The testosterone level around here has been unbearable." Although they'd only met once, she hugged Kenzie. "It's nice to see you again, Kenzie." She glanced at the pie box in Kenzie's hands. "You stopped at Sugar and Spice. Did you get any of their seven-layer magic bars?"

"They didn't have any today," Kenzie answered. "If they had, I would have gotten a few. They're one of my favorites."

"Is Alex not coming today?" Ryan asked. He'd hoped she'd be here today. A lover of all things plant, he thought she and Kenzie would get along well.

Mad Dog shook her head. "I'm not sure she and Matt are back."

The previous week, Alex and Matt had headed down to South America to help a high-ranking Chinese official defect to the United States. If Mad Dog hadn't heard from Alex, they must not be back. As the only two women on HRT, they'd developed a strong bond.

"Jen, I want to be there." Keith's words caught both Ryan's attention and Mad Dog's. "I can get the next flight up and meet you at your house," Keith continued, running a hand through his hair. "If you change your mind, call me." Ending the call, he looked at Mad Dog, and then as if just remembering they weren't alone, he nodded in Ryan and Kenzie's direction. "Hey."

"Is everyone okay?" Ryan asked. If someone in his family were sick or injured, he'd want to be there for them too.

"The media is running a bullshit story about Jen. Something they probably got from one of Brett's opponents."

"And your sister doesn't want you to come home?" Ryan asked.

"No." Crossing his arms, Keith leaned against the counter.

"You could still go." Mad Dog added the final wing to the platter as she continued. "I can bring you home so you can pack a bag and then drop you off at the airport."

He'd noticed Keith's car wasn't out front when they pulled up but had assumed the guy hadn't arrived. Judging by the conversation between Mad Dog and Keith, they'd arrived together. Did that mean Keith had gotten his head on straight and asked Mad Dog out? If he had, it was about damn time.

"Jen's upset enough. If I show up after she told me not to, it'll only piss her off more," Keith answered with frustration.

Mad Dog feigned a shocked expression and pressed her hand against her chest. "You're actually doing what your sister told you to do? I think I need to mark this down somewhere. It might never happen again." After a moment, her expression grew serious again, and she touched Keith's hand. "The Sherbrookes are used to dealing with the media. I'm sure Jen has all the help she needs."

Kenzie's eyebrows went up at the name Sherbrooke. Later he'd have to explain.

"I'm going to bring the wings outside," Mad Dog said.

"Are you coming back in?" Ryan asked.

With a nod, she grabbed the platter off the counter. "Leaving Kenzie alone with the two of you would be cruel and unusual punishment." She shot Kenzie a look. "I have a lot to share with you that I'm sure Salty hasn't told you."

THIRTEEN

A week later, Kenzie found herself seated at her favorite place for lunch. Stabbing a cherry tomato, she shifted in her seat as she glanced around the outdoor patio. As usual, people eating lunch before they headed back to work or whatever other plans they had for the afternoon filled the restaurant down the street from Parkview Immediate Care. Even though she and Mary Ellen, a nurse at the clinic, had taken a later than usual lunch, every table both inside and outside was occupied. And as far as she could tell, everyone was either paying attention to their meals, their cell phones, or, in a few rare cases, their lunch companions. Still, she couldn't shake the feeling someone was watching her. It wasn't the first time this week she'd experienced it either.

Yesterday when she took Marley out for his morning walk, she'd felt watched. Even though she hadn't seen or heard anyone around her, she'd cut their walk short and headed back to the house. Then last night on her drive home, the same dark-colored SUV had been behind her for much of the trip. Worried it was following her, Kenzie took the long way to her neighborhood because it would eventually bring her past the police station. If the car was still there by the time she reached the station, she could pull into their parking lot and call for help. The detour turned out to be been unnecessary, and after the car turned and headed in a different direction, she chastised herself and her overactive imagination. After all, who would want to follow her? She wasn't a famous actress or rich heiress. Despite telling herself it'd all been her imagination, she'd skipped taking Marley for a walk when she got home and double-checked to make sure she'd locked all the doors and windows before going to bed. She'd been living alone since graduating from college, but last night for the first time since then she wished she had a roommate.

By this morning, though, common sense had returned, and she took Marley for his usual walk before jumping in the shower and heading for work. Unlike on the drive home yesterday, no one single car had remained behind her, further convincing her that her imagination had just been running wild the previous day.

Unfortunately, the darn thing was at work again. Since nothing on the patio explained the unease tying her stomach in knots, she switched her gaze to the outdoor patio of the restaurant next door. She didn't know about inside, but it looked like all the tables and all the seats at the outdoor bar over there were full too.

Bringing her fork to her mouth, Kenzie scanned the tables she could see from her seat. Much like the customers seated around her, the ones at the other restaurant seemed occupied with their lunches and friends. Without paying attention to her food, she stabbed her salad and switched her gaze to the benches along the sidewalk.

Her eyes froze on the man standing with one leg propped up on the bench while he ate a sub from one of the nearby sandwich shops.

"Hey, are you still with me?" Mary Ellen waved a hand

near Kenzie's face, and she blinked before forcing her eyes away from the man who'd caught her attention.

"Sorry. I got distracted." Setting her fork down, she scooted her chair closer and lowered her voice. "I think someone is watching us." She felt stupid even uttering the words, but maybe Mary Ellen could convince her once and for all she was imagining things.

Mary Ellen leaned closer before speaking. "Where are they?"

"On the sidewalk. The guy wearing jeans and standing by the bench eating." She nodded slightly in his direction but otherwise kept her eyes focused on the building across the street.

A group of businessmen, most of whom were paying more attention to their phones than each other, passed by, momentarily blocking their view of the man in question. "He's kind of cute," Mary Ellen replied once the group passed.

"I tell you I think he's watching us, and you think he's cute?"

"Some of us don't have a handsome neighbor who takes us to look at flowers and to baseball games." She glanced at Kenzie briefly before looking back at the man again. "I'm not sure. It's possible he's looking in our direction." Mary Ellen shrugged before reaching for her lemonade. "Maybe he likes what he sees. If he comes over and asks for my phone number, I'll consider giving it to him. But considering my luck lately, he'll ask for yours instead."

If luck existed, Mary Ellen had been on the receiving end of nothing but bad luck for the past several months, starting in February when someone stole her new car. Kenzie hoped her friend's most recent mishap, having to replace the hot water heater at her house three weeks ago, was Mary Ellen's last problem for a long time.

Kenzie dragged her attention back to her lunch and took another forkful of salad. "I don't know why, but he's making me uncomfortable. I wish he'd finish his lunch and leave."

"Until he does, how about we pretend he isn't there?"

Easier said than done, but she'd try.

"Since you didn't seem to hear my question before, I'll ask you again. Are things still great with Ryan, or has he finally started to show you all his bad habits?"

The word great was a poor way to describe their relationship. "I haven't seen any bad habits yet, but he's been away since Wednesday. So who knows?"

"Business trip?" Mary Ellen asked, reaching for the salt.

Ryan had never told her not to tell anyone what he did, and thanks to some of its high-profile clients, most people across the country recognized the name Elite Force Security. "I guess you could call it that. He works for Elite Force Security. The private security firm in Alexandria."

"That's kind of cool. So what do they have him doing now? Following around one of those reality stars?"

Kenzie shook her head as her eyes darted back to the bench again. Sure enough, Mr. I-Eat-My-Lunch-Standing-Up was still there. "Have you heard anything about the Colby Gibson murder trial in Beverly Hills?" Except for the special election up in Massachusetts, the media had been obsessed with little else for the past few weeks. Especially since Colby Gibson was the eldest son of a big-name movie producer.

"Who hasn't?"

"One of the prosecution's witnesses is the daughter of some mega-rich businessman from France. He hired the firm to stay with his daughter until she returns home."

"She witnessed the murder? I don't remember the media mentioning that there were any witnesses to what happened that night."

"No, I read somewhere she was at the party earlier in the

evening. Supposedly she also spent a lot of time with the couple when they were dating and saw Gibson get violent with Monica several times."

"Doesn't sound like a person who needs a bodyguard following her around. It's not like she's testifying in a mob case or something."

She'd had a similar thought when Ryan called her Wednesday morning and explained he was headed to California because Christian was sick and unable to cover the assignment. "Maybe it makes her feel better. I imagine testifying in any kind of murder trial can be unsettling. Or maybe it makes her parents feel better. Who knows?"

"A bodyguard, huh? I definitely wouldn't want a job that forces me to put my life in danger for the sake of someone else."

Kenzie knew Ryan did more than just act as a bodyguard. He hadn't gone into specifics, but he'd explained he'd worked on a few missing person cases too. "You and me both."

"When does he get back?" Mary Ellen stabbed the last french fry on her plate and dipped it in ketchup.

"His plane is supposed to arrive at seven thirty, but you never know. He promised to call me once he's on his way home." She'd flown enough to know all types of things caused delays when it came to air travel, and an arrival time was just an estimate.

Pushing her empty plate away, Mary Ellen glanced at the sidewalk—a place Kenzie was forcing herself not to look at again. "Our friend left."

Immediately, she lifted her head. Two children eating donuts and a woman she guessed was their grandmother had replaced the man from earlier. Relief spread through her body, and she could practically feel the knots in her stomach uncoil.

"If you don't have any plans until Ryan gets home, do you want to come shopping with me? I need to get a dress for a wedding I'm going to this weekend, and if I have some company, it'll make the experience almost tolerable."

She'd gone shopping with Mary Ellen before. The woman was the most efficient shopper she'd ever seen. Her friend went in with an idea of what she wanted and shopped only for that. She didn't get distracted by window displays or the need to fill her closet with shoes and handbags she didn't really need, unlike Megan, who couldn't see a sale and not pick something up regardless of whether or not she needed it. So if they went to the mall right from work, most likely Kenzie would be home before Ryan's plane even landed.

"Sure."

"I've been meaning to ask you. What do you think of the new X-ray tech, Gerard? We're supposed to have dinner together tomorrow night."

Looked like Mary Ellen's bad luck was still going strong. "He's married."

Confusion replaced her smile. "How do you know? He doesn't wear a ring."

For a reason, she suspected. Since she'd started at Parkview in the spring, she'd overheard him asking out Desiree, another nurse at the clinic, and she'd seen him kissing the phlebotomist in the parking lot—a woman Kenzie knew for a fact wasn't his wife.

"I passed by him and Bryan outside while they were smoking a couple of weeks ago, and I heard Bryan ask him how his wife was feeling. Gerard said he was happy to announce she no longer had morning sickness."

Mary Ellen huffed and tossed her napkin down. "I can't believe he has a pregnant wife, and he asked me out. Talk about a grade-A scumbag. Looks like my bad luck strikes again. Any chance Ryan has any single brothers or friends you can introduce me to?"

His brothers were too far away, and his friends Connor and Keith were both in relationships. Well, she thought Keith and Maddie were together. They'd spent much of the cookout near each other, and more than once she saw them off together talking. At the same time, though, she hadn't seen them touch once. No handholding or an arm around the shoulders, unlike Connor and his girlfriend, Becca, who were joined at the hip the entire night, and they certainly hadn't been shy about public displays of affection. But Connor and Keith weren't Ryan's only friends. "I'll talk to Ryan and get back to you."

Twenty minutes and she could call it a day. Man, what a day it'd turned out to be. The morning had been slow, with only one patient in the clinic at a time, and except for a high-school-aged girl who Kenzie diagnosed with mono and a retired elementary school teacher with bronchitis, everyone she saw in the morning was either suffering from allergies or the common cold. After lunch, the clinic had been a far different place. At one point every room was occupied with patients suffering from everything from twisted ankles and deep cuts requiring stitches to crying toddlers with ear infections. Then there had been the woman who came in with all the symptoms of a heart attack and they had to rush her to the emergency room by ambulance. It'd been so busy she hadn't even had time to use the restroom. She was pretty sure Tiffany, the other physician's assistant working today, hadn't either.

For the first time since lunch, Kenzie dropped into her chair and grabbed the bottle of water on her desk. With the nonstop string of patients, she hadn't been able to check her phone. Now seemed like a good time to see if she'd missed any calls or received any messages. Pulling out the device, she unlocked the screen. Sure enough, she'd missed two calls, but since neither were from people in her contact list and the callers hadn't bothered to leave voice mail messages, she assumed they were both junk calls. It seemed like she was getting more and more of them every week. Besides the phone calls, she'd received a text message from Ryan.

My connecting flight out of Chicago is delayed by an hour. I'll let you know when I'm on my way.

As far as delays went, an hour wasn't too bad.

Although he wouldn't see it until after he landed, she sent back a message and put her phone back in the desk drawer.

"Kenzie, the patient in room four is asking to be seen by you instead of Tiffany," Mary Ellen said after knocking on the office door.

It hadn't taken long for Kenzie to learn the clinic had at least a dozen regulars, patients who used it rather than visit a primary care doctor whenever they were sick. And like with most things, some of them preferred to be seen by certain providers if possible. Most of the regulars she didn't mind seeing, but there were some she cringed when she saw their name on the intake form.

"Which one of our friends is it?" After taking one last sip of water, Kenzie stood.

Mary Ellen handed her the clipboard with the intake information. "He doesn't look familiar to me, but he asked if it was possible to see you."

Just because her friend didn't recognize the man didn't mean he wasn't a patient she hadn't treated fifty times before. While they often worked together during the week, Mary Ellen never worked weekends. Kenzie glanced at the name on the form. Gabriel Wilson didn't ring any bells.

"Let's hope he's just suffering from a cold or allergies," she said as she walked away.

Gabriel flipped through the six-month-old travel magazine. It'd been that or one of the fashion magazines he snagged out of the rack on the wall. He'd toyed with the idea of coming here ever since he opened the files the private investigator gave him and he learned where Kenzie Armstrong lived and worked. Repeatedly he'd told himself it wasn't necessary. Jax had been following her since the previous Tuesday afternoon, learning her daily routine as well as identifying if there were any people she regularly came in contact with. While he'd been busy with that, Shawn had continued to follow Armstrong's wife. Since he'd be calling Armstrong once he had the guy's wife and daughter, it seemed a waste of time and, more importantly, money to have him followed any longer. Although neither man had given him formal reports on the two women's routines, both had updated him as to their plans.

Over the past few days, the only person Jax had seen enter or leave the house was Kenzie, confirming that she lived alone, so he'd decided the best place to get her was at home after she'd gone to bed for the night. He'd already determined she didn't have an alarm system or any cameras outside, and he'd assured Gabe picking the door locks would be easy. Once inside the house, Jax would tie her up and move her to the trunk of her car. Then he'd leave in her vehicle, eliminating the need to carry her outside and risk someone seeing them. Eventually, when she didn't show up for work, her coworkers would grow suspicious. If a police officer stopped by to do a welfare check, they'd find her car gone and perhaps initially assume she'd left on her own.

Unfortunately, the plan wouldn't work with the wife.

Even if Shawn got into the house without setting off the security system, he'd have to deal with an armed former FBI agent who trained people to defend themselves, which might result in Edward Armstrong's premature death. Instead, Shawn and Carles would take the woman from her photography studio after her part-time assistant left for the day. The location meant the possibility they'd be seen was greater for them than for Jax, but it was the only time and place they could confirm she'd be alone.

Much like when he'd hung out at the café across from Armstrong's self-defense and firearms school, his curiosity finally won out. Unlike the day he'd staked out Protection First though, he wasn't worried about Kenzie Armstrong recognizing him—or his name, for that matter. If the FBI had been able to prove the full extent of his insider trading activities, his arrest and trial might have garnered media attention, especially if it had been a slow month in terms of news. While Gabe didn't doubt Armstrong had tried, he had only been able to prove Gabe hacked into the CEO of Sagewood Technologies' computer files and then used the information he gathered to make trades on the stock market. So, although he'd served a few years and the government had acquired a fraction of his funds, a substantial portion of the small fortune he'd built up still belonged to him even after the divorce settlement Savannah received.

A knock sounded at the door, and Gabe tossed the old magazine onto the nearby chair. Finally, he was going to meet Edward Armstrong's only daughter. The one he'd take away from the man forever just like Armstrong had done to him. "Come on in."

The photos Sam provided hadn't done justice to the woman in front of him. Perhaps five feet three, with dirty-blonde hair and amazing eyes, she wasn't the type of woman a guy would forget. It was too bad she had to die.

"Mr. Wilson." She closed the door behind her and put the clipboard she held down on the counter. "One of the nurses said you asked for me."

Her statement sounded more like a question. She wanted to know how he knew her. He'd expected that even before he walked into the lobby. "Last fall you treated my daughter when I brought her in with a sprained wrist. She was a mess, but you did a great job calming her down and getting her to cooperate for X-rays. I was in again this past spring when she had an ear infection and the provider we saw was nothing like you."

There was no way Kenzie remembered every patient she treated, and everyone liked compliments. Even his brother liked it when he pointed out the things he did well in the ring. So there was no reason Kenzie would be any different.

Her stance changed, and she seemed to relax. "I'm glad I could make her experience less stressful. The nurse said you have a sore throat. How long has it been bothering you?"

"A few days. And I've had a sinus headache since yesterday."

She jotted notes on the clipboard. After getting a tongue depressor from the jar, she removed the otoscope from the wall. "I've seen several cases of strep this week, so I recommend doing a strep test."

The thing would come back negative, but he played along. "You're the expert here. Whatever you feel is best."

FOURTEEN

As Kenzie expected, her trip to the mall with Mary Ellen was short and sweet. Her friend entered the mall not only knowing what style of dress she wanted but which stores she wanted to visit. They struck out in the first two, but number three proved to be the charm. Not only had Mary Ellen found one empire-waist-style dress in a color she liked, she found four, meaning it'd taken slightly longer than usual for her to exit the dressing room and make her purchase. Kenzie hadn't been surprised when she settled on the one that matched shoes she already had at home, eliminating the need to spend any more time at the mall.

Starting from the moment she left work and throughout the time she spent in the mall, Kenzie kept an eye out for anyone who seemed to be following her. While she had no reason to believe the guy near the bench had been watching them, she figured it never hurt to be extra vigilant while they walked around. Unlike at lunch, no one caught her attention, and unlike on her walk with Marley, she didn't get the sense anyone was following her. That didn't stop her from glancing in the rearview mirror more times than necessary as she drove from the mall to Giovanni's Pizza to pick up her takeout order, and then again on the way home.

For a few minutes during the ride from Giovanni's to her neighborhood, a bright red pickup truck had stayed behind her, once again setting off warning bells. But it turned into a gas station a few blocks from the restaurant, and she never saw it again, which meant Kenzie was once again chastising her overactive imagination when she entered the kitchen and closed the door leading into the garage behind her.

Marley's bark greeted her before she reached the laundry room in the basement, aka his bedroom when she wasn't home.

"Hey there, buddy." She moved the baby gate she used, rather than shut the door, to keep the dog from leaving the room. Immediately the dog stopped barking and walked over to her, his tail wagging a mile a minute.

After switching off the laundry room light, Kenzie scratched Marley under his collar. "Ready to eat?" At the word *eat*, the dog trotted off toward the stairs. He paused once and looked back at her as if to make sure she was following him and then continued on.

The scent of pizza filled the kitchen, and Marley parked himself near the counter rather than his dog bowl. More often than not when she ordered pizza, the dog found himself on the receiving end of some. She didn't doubt the same would happen tonight. "I'm hungry too, Marley, but the pizza is for later."

The dog remained unfazed by the comment. He didn't even move when Kenzie opened the closet where she kept the airtight container of dry dog food. Usually, he followed her right in when he knew it was time to eat. Clearly, the smell of the eggplant parmesan pizza, one of her favorites, and the meat lovers, Ryan's preferred type, was too much for him to ignore. She didn't blame him. The dry food she fed him every day might be from one of the best dog food brands out there, and she switched up the flavors she purchased, but it had to be boring to eat the same thing day in and day out.

"I'll share with you later. I promise. If you're lucky, maybe Ryan will too." She added the food to his bowl, and at the sound of the kibble hitting the plastic, Marley left his post near the counter. At least for the time being. Once he finished inhaling his dinner, he'd go back to guarding the pizzas and hoping one somehow miraculously fell to the floor.

Starving or not, she'd wait until Ryan arrived to dig into dinner, but she would not wait for him to have a drink. Not after the crazy-busy afternoon she'd had. Popping the cap off an alcohol-infused bottle of root beer, something she'd only discovered existed this past spring, she took a sip as she kicked off her leather clogs.

Although it wasn't what he wanted, Marley devoured his food and followed her from the room. Ryan had sent a text message while he waited at baggage claim, saying he'd be over after he dropped off his stuff next door. That had been about forty-five minutes ago, so assuming he didn't hit too much traffic, he should there soon. Before he arrived, she wanted a quick shower, because although she put on extra deodorant and changed before heading to the mall, she felt icky. While no doubt the shower would be much more fun with Ryan, she didn't want to greet him as she was. Besides, it wasn't like they couldn't enjoy some time in the shower later tonight or tomorrow morning.

Glad to be home, Ryan dropped his suitcase near the bed and switched off the light on his way out of the room. While he didn't mind traveling for work, he preferred when it didn't involve flying. Business class or not, airplane seats were not designed for adult males. Hell, they weren't designed for adult females either. If he had to guess, he'd say the only people who could fit in them comfortably were preadolescent kids. Add to that the frequent need for connecting flights and the delays that often popped up, and air travel could be more unpleasant than an interrogation. Unfortunately, until someone invented a way to beam a person from one place to another like in his favorite science-fiction series, it was the quickest way to travel across long distances, something he did much more frequently with Elite Force than he ever did when he worked for the FBI. It was perhaps the biggest drawback to his current line of work. All things considered, though, he'd rather work for the firm than anyone else.

He and Kenzie had talked a few times while he'd been in California and exchanged text messages, but all the calls had been short. Between the time difference and the fact he needed to stick by Elaina Brodeur every time she left her hotel room, long conversations had been impossible. Tonight, he was looking forward to simply sitting next to Kenzie and talking. Sure, it wasn't the only thing he was looking forward to, but unlike with other women he'd spent time with, he enjoyed hearing about how her day had been or whatever else was on her mind, and he enjoyed having someone to share his thoughts with.

Marley's usual greeting didn't erupt inside the house after he rang the doorbell, meaning either Kenzie wasn't home and the dog was still in the basement, or he was outside. He was about to ring the bell a second time when the door opened.

Kenzie's hair hung loose, the way he preferred it around her shoulders. Droplets of water clung to her tanned shoulders, and one tantalizing droplet was slipping over her clavicle toward the neckline of her tank top. "Good timing. I just got out of the shower."

"Good timing would have been if I arrived before you got in so I could have joined you." In one movement, Ryan closed the door and pulled her close. Lowering his head, he licked the water droplets off her right shoulder before kissing it. Then he repeated the action on her left side. "If you'd waited, I would have washed your back for you."

Slipping his hands under her shirt, he ran them up her back and then down again before disappearing under the waistband of her old cutoffs. With her tight ass in his hands, his dick grew harder.

"Trust me, it's better I didn't wait. But if you feel you need a shower before we eat, I'll happily wash your back for you." Taking his earlobe between her lips, she tugged on it, sending any blood still elsewhere in his body straight to his dick.

He took her against the shower wall before she even finished washing his legs. Afterward, they found their way to Kenzie's bed, where he devoted his attention to every part of her body before entering her. They'd orgasmed almost simultaneously. He would have been happy to stay naked and in her bedroom until tomorrow morning, but his belly had other ideas. Judging by the sounds Kenzie's stomach made, hers didn't want to lounge around in bed either. When they came downstairs, they found Marley sitting on the back step waiting to come inside. The dog hadn't left them since they carried the pizzas into the living room and sat down to eat.

"How did it go in LA?" Kenzie fed the rest of her pizza crust to Marley and then added a second slice of eggplant parmesan pizza to her plate.

Although no longer hot, the pizza she'd picked up from Giovanni's was the best-tasting thing he'd had all day. "Much the way I expected. I kept a few reporters from bothering her, but otherwise she didn't need private security. I was more or less an expensive babysitter whenever Elaina left her hotel suite, and then I made sure she got on her flight back to France early this morning."

She plucked a slice of eggplant off her pizza and popped it in her mouth before licking some sauce off her fingers. The innocent action immediately brought back the memory of where her tongue and mouth had been while she worked on washing his thighs. On cue, his stupid dick got ready for round three. This time, though, it'd have to wait.

"Do you think they'll find Colby guilty? At least according to what the media has printed, he certainly sounds it."

Ryan slammed the door on the images and focused on her question. He agreed with Kenzie, especially after what he'd heard while in the courtroom this week. However, Elaina was the last witness for the prosecution before the defense called theirs, so who knew what information he'd missed or what ace the defense might have up their sleeve. "If I was on the jury, I sure as hell would. But who knows, he's got some of the best attorneys money can buy. And we both know juries have let off guys like him before even when the evidence against them is overwhelming." It wouldn't surprise him to read they'd found him not guilty when the trial ended.

If Kenzie wanted the boring specifics about his time in Los Angeles, he'd share them later. Right now, he'd rather hear about what she'd been up to while he was away. "How was your week?" Ryan took a swig from his beer and added another two slices of pizza to his plate.

"Normal, I guess." She shrugged a shoulder and reached for her drink.

Her tone made it impossible for him to accept her answer without further clarification. "You guess? Did something happen at work?" She'd never complained about her coworkers, but no matter where you worked, you ran into jerks. He didn't see any reason Parkview would be any different.

As if stalling, she raised her glass to her lips and took a sip rather than answer him. "Work was work. Some days it was one patient after another, and others it was slow." She took her time putting the glass down and wiping her mouth with a paper napkin.

Based on the days she'd described to him in the past, her week sounded fairly standard to him, so what was up with her earlier answer? "You're not telling me something, Kenzie. I can hear it in your voice." He'd learned quickly that a person's tone, facial expressions, and body language could be even more important than their words.

"You'll think I've lost it."

"Believe me, it's too late for that. I've heard the full conversations you have with Marley while you garden."

She cracked a smile and poked him in the arm. "More than once I've heard you talking to Marley when you're here."

At the sound of his name, the dog put his front paws up on her thigh and stared at Kenzie, his eyes willing her to give up more pizza. Like a charm, the pathetic look worked, and she broke off a corner from a slice and gave it to him. With his prize in his mouth, Marley dropped back to the floor and got to work.

"Just trying to stay on his good side so he doesn't pee on my shoes in the middle of the night," Ryan explained. "So what happened this week?"

"Fine. But you better not laugh when I tell you. Yesterday morning I got this weird feeling when I took Marley for his walk. Kind of like someone was watching me. And last night I thought a car was following me home, but it eventually turned in a different direction."

Following a person and not being seen took skill and practice. He should know. "Did you see anyone around?"

Shaking her head, Kenzie tore another corner off her pizza and fed it to Marley, who'd come back looking for seconds. "No, but I skipped our walk last night anyway."

"What about this morning? Did you get the same feeling?"

"No. I got it a little again while Mary Ellen and I were out for lunch, but eventually it went away."

He didn't know who Mary Ellen was. Except for her cousin, he'd met none of her friends or coworkers. "You're sure there wasn't anyone around either time." Sometimes a person's imagination got the better of them, made them feel or even see things that weren't really there. Other times, feelings like Kenzie experienced were the brain's way of saying something about a situation or an environment was wrong or dangerous. Unfortunately, people rarely knew which was the case until it was too late.

With her pizza almost to her mouth, Kenzie's hand stopped. "I'm positive I didn't see anyone while Marley and I were walking. And believe me, I checked. At lunch, there was a guy near a bench eating, and he might have been looking in our direction. Mary Ellen and I weren't positive. But he never came inside the restaurant, and he walked away before we left to go back to work."

A guy checking out women while he ate his lunch wasn't unusual. He'd done it, as had every guy he knew.

"You don't have to say it. It's all in my head. I know. I think I've been on a mystery kick too long. It's time to switch back to romance novels for a few months."

"I wasn't going to." With two sisters and numerous female cousins, he knew when to keep his trap shut.

"But you were thinking it."

Based on the evidence, yeah, he was. "Whether or not it's

your imagination, it never hurts to pay attention to your surroundings."

"Why am I not surprised you sound like my father?" she asked before wiping her hands on a napkin and reaching for her drink. "Okay, I think it's time to change the subject. What's the deal between Maddie and Keith? It definitely seemed like there was something going on between them at Spike's house."

Good question. He'd gotten a similar impression and had watched them on and off all night. Unfortunately, nothing about their behavior confirmed 100 percent that the relationship between them had changed.

"No idea."

"Come on, Ryan. You work with both of them. How can you not know if they're together?"

"Keith's had it bad for Mad Dog for months. Maybe he finally did something about it. If he did, he didn't share the details with me." Mad Dog and Keith had left the cookout together the previous week, and Ryan hadn't had a chance to talk much to either of them since.

"Keith doesn't seem like the type to be shy about asking women out."

Kenzie was right. "He's not shy when it comes to anything." Keith never admitted it, but Ryan assumed that was part of the problem. Since he'd never had a problem sharing how and with whom he spent his free time, Mad Dog knew Keith rarely saw the same woman more than a few times. On more than one occasion, she'd let them all know what she thought of men like Keith.

"Well, assuming Keith and Maddie are together, besides Spike, do you have any other single friends?"

"Looking to replace me?"

Reaching out, she patted him on the hand and gifted him with one of her sucker-punch smiles. "Don't worry. You're safe for now anyway. I thought we could play matchmaker and set one of your friends up with my friend Mary Ellen. She's a nurse I work with. When it comes to men, she has the worst luck. Maybe the four of us can go out on a double date."

Ryan cringed at the word matchmaker. He'd been on the receiving end of his older sister's various matchmaking attempts. Despite Vanessa's best intentions, none had ended well. At least not for him. Thanks to Vanessa's need to play Cupid, his eldest brother Kyle had met his wife.

Before he possibly subjected one of his friends to a date from hell, he needed more information. "Tell me a little about her, and I'll let you know if she'd get along with anyone I know."

FIFTEEN

Ryan pulled into the unusually wide driveway of a house at least twice the size of the one she'd grown up in. Then again, a family of eight people needed something bigger than a family of three. A basketball hoop stood off to the right. Someone had painted the paved area underneath the hoop blue, with the three-point arc, the free-throw line, the free-throw lane, and a giant S painted white. She imagined Ryan and his siblings had played countless games in the driveway with their friends. A stone porch extended across the front of the house and wrapped around one side. White wicker furniture and colorful flowering plants decorated it. Kenzie wondered if Ryan's family ever sat out there or if the furniture was there simply as decoration. The Austens, her parents' next-door neighbors, had a smaller but very similar porch on their house, but they never used the patio furniture on it.

"Looks like almost everyone is already here," Ryan commented as he turned the car off and opened his door. "Mom wasn't sure if my grandparents would make it today. I'm glad they did."

Kenzie blinked and looked around as she got out of the

car, not the easiest of tasks considering she was eight months pregnant. Although the driveway had been empty before, now there were four other cars parked near them. Another was parked at the street along with a motorcycle.

A man who had to be Ryan's dad, judging by the resemblance, exited the house and waved as he headed toward the car. A moment later, an attractive woman perhaps in her early sixties followed.

"It's about time we met your fiancée, Ryan." The woman hugged Ryan first and then turned her attention toward Kenzie. "I was starting to think we weren't going to meet you until the wedding in the spring. How have you been feeling?"

Kenzie opened her mouth to answer, but an odd sound she couldn't quite identify filled the air. "What is that?" The sound came again, pulling at Kenzie's memory. Nails scratching against fabric.

The vision of Ryan's house and family disappeared as Kenzie slowly woke up. The sound was Marley scratching the sheet on the bed. After he'd gone outside for the last time, he'd reluctantly curled up on his bed under the windows and soon started snoring.

Opening her eyes, she reached out and touched the dog's head and tried to clear both the sleep and memories of her dream from her head. It'd been one of the crazier ones she had in a long time. Perhaps eating a large bowl of death by chocolate ice cream topped with whipped cream and hot fudge right before bed wasn't the best of ideas. Regardless of whether or not it had been a bad idea, it had tasted delicious and satisfied the craving for something sweet she'd had all day.

Although the temperature during the day still reached into the eighties and even sometimes into the nineties, ever since the calendar had changed to September, the evenings had become cooler. In fact, she'd turned the central air conditioner off before going up to bed most nights and just left her bedroom windows open and the ceiling fan on instead. When they'd gone up to bed tonight, they'd opted to do the same thing. Now the sound of crickets floated in through the open window, along with the sound of a car.

The dog scratched the bed again and nudged her hand with his nose. Most of the time Marley slept through the night, but occasionally he needed to go outside. Before he started barking, which would be his next move if she ignored him, and woke Ryan up, she pushed back the sheet and swung her legs out of bed. Marley sprinted off toward the closed bedroom door.

"Is everything okay?" Ryan asked from behind her.

Kenzie leaned over and kissed his cheek. "Sorry, I was trying not to wake you. Marley needs to go out."

"You didn't. I've been up for a good ten minutes. I was about to go downstairs and get a snack. I can let him out." He didn't wait for an answer. Instead, he kicked off the sheet covering the lower half of his body and stood. "Do you want me to bring you anything?" he asked as he pulled on his shorts.

Between all the pizza and the ice cream, she didn't think she'd be hungry for breakfast, never mind a snack now. She could use a drink though. Kenzie loved pizza, but it, much like tacos, made her unusually thirsty.

"I'll come down with you and grab some water."

Marley took off when she opened the door. Kenzie knew from experience he'd stop when he reached the top of the stairs and wait to make sure she was coming. If the dog was anything, it was predictable. She didn't bother to turn the hallway light on. Between the window at the end of the hall and the skylight in the ceiling, more than enough moonlight came in to make their way to the stairs.

The dog waited until they caught up with him before

continuing on. When they reached the bottom of the stairs, she flipped up the light switch and froze. Her brain struggled to process the fact a man was in her kitchen, just a handful of steps from the back door. Dressed all in black, including his gloves, he had a shaved head, making it impossible to determine his hair color, and a backpack slung over one shoulder.

Although she remained rooted in place, Ryan and Marley weren't. As soon as the light went on, Marley started barking and charged forward. Ryan reacted just as quickly, minus the barking.

"Go upstairs. Lock the door and call the police," Ryan shouted as he ran toward the kitchen and the guy who was already opening the back door while Marley tried to bite him through his jeans.

Yelp. Marley cried out as he went flying across the floor.

She didn't see any weapons in his hands, but it didn't mean her unwelcome visitor didn't have a gun or knife on him. She'd rather have the intruder escape than have Ryan injured or worse.

Ignoring his command to go upstairs, she sprinted across the house, past Marley, who was getting up, thank God, and grabbed the cordless phone on the counter. Several times since she'd moved in she'd thought about getting rid of her landline. Now she was glad she hadn't, because she could call the police without going upstairs to get her cell.

"Ryan!" She didn't care if she woke the entire neighborhood tonight.

Marley tried to rush past her and outside, but she grabbed him by the collar. He didn't seem hurt despite being kicked. If he caught up with the creep, he might not be so lucky again.

"911 what is the nature of your emergency?" the dispatcher asked when he answered the call.

. . .

Ryan chased the intruder through the gate and into the driveway.

"Ryan!"

Damn it. He'd told her to go upstairs and call the police. For half a heartbeat, his feet slowed, allowing the intruder to reach the street.

"Ryan," Kenzie called out again.

Despite the other guy's head start, Ryan knew he could still catch him. But then what? He had no handcuffs, no zip ties, and no cell phone. Hell, he didn't even have any shoes on. If he overtook him, then what? Was he supposed to ask the jerk to use his phone to call the police? Sit on him until the cops arrived?

Being there for Kenzie was more important than catching some punk looking to steal whatever he could get his hands on. Ryan watched the guy jump into a car stopped at the corner with its lights turned off. Except for the fact it was a dark-colored SUV, he couldn't identify the make and model. Not exactly a lot to give the police when they showed up.

Turning, Ryan headed back to the house, not sure what kind of condition he'd find Kenzie in. Put in a similar circumstance, his younger sister would be a hysterical mess, while his mom and older sister would be pissed someone had forced their way inside.

Marley launched into his usual greeting song when he spotted Ryan. It was a sound Ryan didn't think he'd ever been so happy to hear. If the dog was barking as loudly as usual, his flight through the air hadn't injured him.

After he verified there were no tears streaming down Kenzie's face, Ryan's first instinct was to grab her by the shoulders and shake her. The potential for danger had been low, but not nonexistent. Neither of them had known if the intruder had an accomplice hiding the backyard. "What are you doing out here? I told you to go upstairs."

Kenzie narrowed her eyes at him, a sure sign she didn't like either his tone or comment. She moved the phone away from her mouth so she could answer him. "Talking to the police." She stepped back inside and raised the phone again. "Yes, he's back. Okay, thank you."

She put the phone on the counter and let go of Marley's collar. "The police are on their way." Her eyes swept across him as if looking for any injuries. "You shouldn't have gone after him, Ryan. He might have had a weapon. Are you okay?"

Closing the door behind him, he walked toward her. "I'm fi—"

"You're bleeding."

Ryan looked down at where she was pointing and the bloody footprints behind him. He didn't remember cutting his foot, but the evidence spoke for itself.

She pulled out a chair and nodded toward it. "Sit down. I'll get the first aid kit."

Despite the unexpected late-night visitor, she appeared calm as she worked to clean and then examine the bottom of his foot. Most people, both men and women, would be on edge after finding a stranger in their kitchen. "What about you? How are you doing?"

"Angry and uneasy," she answered, ripping open a sterile gauze pad. Before she could continue, the doorbell rang, sending Marley straight for the front door. "Here." She held out a roll of medical tape and stood.

"Let me get it."

When he didn't accept the roll, she took his hand and plopped it in his palm. "It's the police. I'll get it. You finish this."

By the time Kenzie escorted the officer into the kitchen, he had the gauze pad secured to his foot.

"I understand that going after him was a gut reaction, but

in situations like this, it's safer to let them get away," Officer Locke commented once they'd finished explaining how they'd come downstairs and found the jerk in the house. "Have either of you seen the intruder around the neighborhood before?"

Ryan shook his head while Kenzie answered, "No."

"Is there anything you can tell me about him? Hair color, height, visible tattoos or piercings?"

"He was about five feet nine with an athletic build. He had a shaved head and a dark tan like someone who spends a lot of time working outside," Kenzie answered. "I didn't see any tattoos."

Officer Locke jotted down the brief description, one that fit countless men. "Anything you can tell me about the car he got into?"

"Only that it was a dark SUV," Ryan answered, annoyed he hadn't been able to get a plate number.

Again the police officer made a note. "There was a similar break-in on Pilgrim Drive last week. The couple came home from a concert and found someone in the house. The intruder got away with several thousand dollars worth of jewelry. And like here, he didn't force open or break any windows. Unfortunately, these days anyone can buy a lock-picking set on the internet, and with enough practice, they can open a lot of the door locks installed on homes."

One of the first things Ryan had done when he moved into his house was upgrade the locks on all the doors. Although they were functional, the contractor who built the home had installed some of the cheapest ones available. Ryan had also had a security system installed within days of moving in.

"My recommendation to you is to have your door locks replaced and consider some type of alarm system. I know this is a safe neighborhood, but it never hurts to have one."

The officer put his pad away and handed them each a business card. "If we learn anything, I will call you. In the meantime, if you have any questions, my extension is on the card."

Ryan stayed in the kitchen with Marley while Kenzie walked Officer Locke to the front door. He didn't need to get a closer look. Even from where he sat, he could tell the lock on the back door was the same cheap brand he'd originally had on his doors. He'd double-check the front door, but he guessed it had a similar one.

Kenzie reentered the room and went straight for the refrigerator. "There's no way I'm going to fall back to sleep. I still can't believe someone got in my house while I was in bed." Pulling out an open bottle of wine, she held it up. "Do you want some?" She didn't wait for an answer; instead, she poured two glasses and carried them over. "If Marley hadn't needed to go out, we might not have known the jerk was here until…." She didn't finish her comment.

He came into the bedroom. Yeah, he'd already thought of that. "Later today I'll replace the locks on your doors. I got rid of the ones the builder installed as soon as I moved in. If you want, I'll give you the name of the company who installed my alarm system. I don't know why they didn't install them when they built these houses."

"Sounds good. I probably should have had one installed after I moved in, but there didn't seem a need. I'll call this morning before I go to work. Hopefully, they can get one in quickly."

Her hand shook so slightly it was barely noticeable, but Ryan saw. Until now, Kenzie had exhibited no signs of how she felt. She didn't need to though. He could see it in her eyes and hear it in her voice.

Whoever the punk had been, Ryan didn't think he'd be back. Still, he'd feel better if Kenzie wasn't alone at night until she had new locks and an alarm. "Until it's in, you and Marley are welcome to stay with me. Or I can stay here."

"Unless you mind, I'd prefer if you stayed here. Marley and Silver don't like change."

He saw her cat so infrequently, he sometimes forgot Kenzie had one. Ryan covered her hand with his. "I'll get everything I need and bring it here later."

Xander knocked on Gabe's office door Tuesday morning and then walked in even though his brother hadn't invited him inside. "We all missed you on Sunday. I thought you were coming up."

Gabe doubted that. Even before his arrest, Xander's in-laws had treated Gabe as if he was just some dumb jock who'd only gotten into Stanford because he could wrestle. The few times he'd seen them since his release from prison, their disdain had been even more obvious. Not that Gabe gave a fuck. So even though he'd told Xander he'd drive out to his lake house for his little get-together, he'd had no intention of going.

"Yeah, sorry. I got busy working out and lost track of time."

"The kids were really disappointed, especially Flynn. He wanted to tell you he scored his first goal for the middle school soccer team last week and show you the new move he's been working on," Xander said, making himself comfortable in the chair opposite Gabe's desk. "I told him I'd invite you to his game today after school. It's a home game. Afterward, you can stop by the house. The weather is supposed to be great. I can grab some steaks and throw them on the grill."

Despite everything, his relationships with Xander and his three kids were still the same as before his arrest. Spending time with his niece and nephews was a double-edged sword. He loved them and enjoyed being with them. At the same time, he couldn't look at them and not think of Logan and Ava.

"What time does it start?" Armstrong's daughter would have competent babysitters until he arrived, but he wanted to be there when they brought in the guy's wife. If the game started early enough, he could catch it, but spending time with Xander and his family would have to wait.

"Three thirty."

"Yeah, I'll be there."

The sound of a car horn came from his desk, and Gabe pulled out the disposable cell phone, hoping to find a message with some good news from Jax. He found the opposite.

I told Shawn to hold off. Things didn't go as planned.

"Fuck." He slammed his fist down on the desk. Jax had promised he'd get the daughter.

What happened?

"Everything okay?" Xander asked.

Glancing up from the screen, he nodded. He'd forgotten his brother was sitting there. "No, my real estate agent just let me know the owners rejected the offer I put in on a house."

"I didn't know you wanted to move," Xander commented as Gabe received another text message.

She wasn't alone. Don't worry, we'll get her.

"Just looking to buy a little vacation place near the beach," he answered while typing another message.

Do it soon.

After sending the response, he put the phone back in his desk drawer.

"Nice. So what about coming over after the game?" Xander unwrapped a stick of gum and then offered Gabe the pack. The guy went through chewing gum like a chain smoker went through cigarettes.

He might as well take Xander up on his offer and stop by the house after the game. "Yeah, I'll come by."

"Before one of the kids announces it or Mom calls and tells you, Lillian is pregnant again. We shared the news with everyone on Sunday."

Gabe's fingers curled around the arm of the chair, his nails digging into the soft leather. Savannah and Gabe had been trying to have another child when Armstrong arrested him. "Congrats, bro. That's great news."

SIXTEEN

Except for the two years after Ryan graduated from college and shared an apartment with Adam and then the three months he'd spent at the FBI academy, he'd lived alone his whole adult life—a situation he'd found he liked. He had no one to answer to, and he had no one complaining when he left his dishes in the kitchen sink or walked through the house without taking his shoes off, something his mom still complained about when he visited her house—his older sister too, for that matter

After a week of staying at Kenzie's house, his view of living alone had changed. He enjoyed being able to reach out at night and pull her close and see her in the morning before they went to work, even if like yesterday it was only for a few minutes. He even looked forward to coming home more, knowing he'd see her and be able to enjoy dinner with company. On Thursday they would start installing Kenzie's new alarm system. The company guaranteed it'd be finished by Friday afternoon, meaning there'd be no reason for him to stay at her house every night. He wasn't looking forward to living alone again.

Ryan made them each another cup of coffee and then let Marley in from the backyard. "What time do you think you'll be home?" Like every Wednesday, Kenzie was working the late shift, which meant she'd be closing the clinic tonight.

"Hopefully it'll be like last week and no one will come in after seven so I can get started on my end of the day reports early. But who knows? As long as the patient comes in by eight, we have to see them."

"Do you want me to stop here and let Marley out before I go to Shooter's?" With Kenzie working late anyway, he'd made plans to meet his friends for a few rounds of pool and a drink at their preferred pub.

She pulled her messy hair into a low ponytail. Although she was up, she didn't need to leave for a few hours, so she hadn't bothered to get ready for the day. "Up to you. I always let him out right before I leave, and he's never had an accident."

Stopping to let Marley out meant he'd drive all of ten minutes out of his way, not exactly a big deal if it meant the dog had a chance to relieve himself. "I'll swing by."

"Still trying to earn brownie points with Marley?"

"Hey, we've become best buds." The dog no longer barked at him, not even when he first entered the house. At night he no longer sat by the side of the bed and glared up at him either. Instead, he curled up on his bed under the window and went to sleep.

"Mmm, I've noticed. I'm sure your willingness to share your food has nothing to do with your new bond." She pointed toward the piece of bacon he was giving the dog. "Who else is going tonight?"

"Keith and Spike. Mad Dog said she might stop by. Do you want me to bring some takeout home for you?"

"Please. I never feel like cooking when I get home on Wednesdays."

Despite the pit stop at Kenzie's house, Ryan got to Shooter's and placed his drink order before any of his friends arrived. He'd never seen the pub empty, and tonight was no different. There wasn't an empty stool at the bar, and he'd snagged the last large booth in the place. Even all the pool tables were being used at the moment.

Before his friends arrived and he got distracted, Ryan sent Kenzie a text message asking what she wanted him to bring her home to eat. Sometimes she answered his texts immediately, other times it took her over an hour.

"Are you sleeping on the couch with the dog yet?" Spike asked, taking a seat across the table from him.

For days Spike had been harassing him with similar comments.

Unless Spike was being quiet about it, he hadn't been in a relationship in months. "At least I have company while I sleep," Ryan answered as Mad Dog slipped into the booth next him. He had to do a double take. A hairdo worthy of a shampoo ad had replaced her usual ponytail. Her hair wasn't the only thing different about her. Wearing a sleeveless dress that knotted at the side, she looked like she'd spent her day working at a bank or law office. While he'd seen her dressed in business attire in the past, those outfits always consisted of dark pants, a button-down shirt, and a blazer. Never had he seen Mad Dog in anything as feminine as her dress. He leaned closer and almost stopped breathing. Mad Dog Dempsey was wearing makeup.

Ryan glanced in Spike's direction. The guy's expression said it all. Mad Dog's new look had thrown him too.

"You made it," Spike said as he reached for one of the menus left by the waitress. "How did the interview go with President Sherbrooke and the First Lady?"

The Sherbrooke family had hired Elite Force Security many times over the years. The most recent time being earlier in the summer when Curt Sherbrooke, the president's nephew, hired them to find his girlfriend's niece after the young girl's biological mother kidnapped her. Now they were hiring the firm to escort the First Lady's mom and her niece when they came to the United States from England in two weeks.

"I see a lot of fundraisers and museums in my future," Mad Dog replied. "They're staying for six weeks."

On the table, Kenzie's name appeared on Ryan's cell phone right before it started to ring.

"Hey, I'd love a bacon cheeseburger with a side of onion rings," Kenzie said.

Odd, but he planned to order almost the same thing for himself. "You got it."

"It's been nonstop in here all day. Hopefully, it will slow down. I'll be home as soon as I can."

He'd hoped so too. "Okay, see you in a couple of hours."

As he finished up his conversation, Keith joined them, taking a seat next to Spike. "Sorry, I'm late." He took the last menu on the table. "There's a bad motorcycle accident a few blocks from here. It must have just happened. Police have the whole street shut down."

Ryan had owned a motorcycle in college. After one too many close calls with other drivers not paying attention, he'd sold it. Every so often he regretted his decision and thought about buying another one, but then he'd hear about or see an accident and the desire would disappear.

Candy, a waitress who'd served them countless times, arrived at their table. "Maddie, this is from the guy at the bar wearing the black T-shirt." She set down a glass of white wine and a slip of paper.

"Thanks." Maddie glanced toward the bar and then picked

up the note. "I'll be right back." Tossing the note on the table, she slipped from the booth.

Since it would be not only immature but also impolite, Ryan refrained from picking up the note and reading it. Instead, he along with everyone else at the table watched Mad Dog cross the pub.

"Do you want to order now, or should I wait until Maddie returns?" Candy asked, reminding everyone at the table she was still there.

"Why don't you come back," Spike answered before looking at his menu again.

"Will do."

Curious as to how Keith felt about some random guy sending Mad Dog drinks, Ryan glanced across the table. Judging by his friend's expression, he didn't like it at all. In fact, he looked ready to tear the guy's arms off. If Mad Dog joined the guy, Ryan wasn't sure how Keith would react.

After a few minutes, she returned.

"Once again you demonstrate that you've got more class than Keith. If a woman bought him a drink, they'd be out the door already," Spike said.

"Maybe I'm meeting up with him later because I'm afraid to leave you three unsupervised."

A muscle in Keith's jaw twitched at her comment.

"Or maybe I already have plans with someone for later tonight." Her eyes darted in Keith's direction, and then she picked up her menu.

Kenzie ignored her rumbling stomach and reached for her lukewarm coffee instead of the emergency cheese crackers stashed in the desk drawer. She had maybe another fifteen minutes of work to finish up. Then she could go home and enjoy a burger and some onion rings, so filling up on crackers seemed silly.

"I finished everything I need to for the night," Desiree said from just inside the office doorway.

Most Wednesday nights, Mary Ellen worked the late shift with Kenzie, while Desiree and Tiffany covered the Tuesday night shift. Once again this week, the two nurses had swapped so Mary Ellen could stay with her mom, who'd undergone surgery the week before, while her dad went to work. Although Desiree was just as competent as Mary Ellen, Kenzie much preferred working with her friend.

"I'm heading out," Desiree continued.

If the nurse had fulfilled her responsibilities, there was no reason for her to stick around and wait for Kenzie. But that never stopped Mary Ellen from offering to stay and keep her company until she finished up what she needed to. "I'm almost done here too. Have a nice night."

"Yeah, you too," Desiree called as she walked away.

With no further interruptions, Kenzie zipped through the last of the reports she needed to complete before powering off the computer. After throwing out the rest of her coffee, she added her cell phone to her pocket and grabbed her wristlet from the desk drawer.

Since the weekend, they'd been experiencing unseasonably high temperatures. After spending the past several hours in a climate-controlled environment, it was like walking into a sauna when she stepped outside.

We'll need the air conditioner tonight.

From the corner of her eye, she spotted a man heading her way as she stepped off the concrete walkway that surrounded the entire building. Immediately, she picked up her pace.

"Hey," the man called out. Although he waved in her direction, Kenzie didn't stop walking. "My car broke down around the corner. Can I borrow your phone?"

Most people carried cell phones. Even her grandmother, a woman two years shy of her ninetieth birthday, had a newer phone than she did, and Nana never left the house without it. If the guy's car had broken down, what were the odds he also didn't have a working phone on him?

Not—

The rest of the thought died in her head as arms wrapped around her from behind and she was pulled against a body as the man who'd asked for her cell phone jogged toward her. For half a heartbeat she froze, paralyzed by fear, and her heart raced, nearly exploding in her chest. Then as if someone flicked a switch, she gained control over her body again. If she didn't get away, there wasn't a doubt in her mind she was as good as dead. It might not happen immediately, but once her kidnappers finished with her, they'd kill her. She'd never studied martial arts formally, but for years her dad had taught her self-defense. It'd been a long time since she practiced with him, but now all the hours of lessons came rushing forward.

Kenzie slammed her head back, hoping to make contact with her kidnapper's nose; then she shifted her body to the left and slammed her fist into her attacker's groin.

"Bitch." For a moment, the arms around her loosened, and she used her bodyweight to break free. If she could just get into her car, she could get away. She only managed a few steps before arms grabbed her again, tighter this time, making it difficult to breathe. Before she could do anything else, he pushed her toward the pavement.

Kenzie hit the ground hard, and the kidnapper's knee pressed into her back, making it impossible to get up. Tears pooled in her eyes, and she opened her mouth to scream, but a hand came down over it. Something bordering on hysteria shot through her, and she tried to buck against the knee holding her down. No matter how hard she tried, she couldn't get the weight to budge as the second kidnapper tied a gag around her mouth before binding her wrists and ankles.

Finally, the pressure on her back disappeared, and she struggled to take in a deep breath through her nose. She heard the beep of a car alarm being turned off, and then one of her kidnappers lifted her off the ground and started walking toward her car.

Thud. Her head hit the jack when she landed inside the trunk. The tears she'd been holding back streamed down her face as the trunk lid slammed closed, engulfing her in darkness. A moment later, she heard a door close, and then the car started to move.

Kenzie never suffered motion sickness. Yet right now, she felt as if she was about to throw up everything she'd eaten for the past week, and that was only one ailment on her list. Sweat was making her clothes stick to her body, and she could no longer feel her hands or feet. Perhaps even worse than having no feeling in her extremities, her chest felt like a boxer had used it as a punching bag thanks to her meeting with the pavement. Swallowing the bile slowly rising in her throat, she closed her eyes and tried to move her hands and feet as much as she could, focusing on her other senses. Judging by the constant movement and the sounds, they were still traveling. She'd never been good at judging time or distance, but it seemed like she'd been in the trunk for an eternity. When she arrived at work this morning, the light indicating the car needed gas was on. Her kidnappers would only get so far with whatever was left, so either they weren't planning to take her far, or they would have to stop and refill. If they did, maybe she could make noise and hopefully draw someone's attention their way. Although at this time of night, it was possible there wouldn't be anyone else at the gas station.

In her back pocket, her phone started ringing. The caller

had to be Ryan. She didn't know what time it was, but she'd powered off her computer around eight thirty. By now Ryan was probably at the house wondering where she was. Kenzie managed to brush her fingers across it, but no matter how hard she tried, she couldn't pull the device from her pocket with her wrists bound. Not that it mattered. Even if she somehow got it out, she couldn't exactly answer it. Eventually, the ringing stopped, as did the movement of the car. Blood thundered in her ears, and her chest tightened.

Pop. The trunk light switched on as it opened, allowing her a good look at the man who'd grabbed her from behind. At first, her brain didn't want to accept what she was seeing. Her kidnapper was the same guy who'd broken into the house the previous week. It hadn't been a random robbery attempt that night.

With her wrists and ankles bound, she couldn't do anything as the kidnapper lifted her out of the car. Surrounded by trees and bushes, the only sounds she could hear were that of nature. There wasn't anything to help her identify their location, and there were no other parked cars around. The headlights of another vehicle shone on them before it came to a stop alongside her car.

The driver emerged as the SUV's liftgate opened. Much the way he'd toss a sack of potatoes, the kidnapper dumped her inside the trunk. Pain shot up her arm, but the gag in her mouth muffled her groan.

Reaching behind her, the goon grabbed the cell phone from her pocket. "You didn't check her pockets." He sounded annoyed as he held the device up.

The driver of the SUV, the same man who'd claimed his car was broken down earlier, didn't seem worried. "Worst case, someone tracks it to this location. So what? Leave it here."

Even as he spoke, the cell phone started ringing again.

"We need to go." The driver of the SUV walked away, and she heard the vehicle's door slam shut.

Jerk number one pulled off his gloves and tossed them in the back with her and then pulled out his cell phone and snapped a picture of her before he slammed the liftgate closed, leaving her trapped in the trunk. A moment or two later, the vehicle started moving. While it might have been her imagination, she swore she felt a slight bump, as if the vehicle had driven over her phone.

Ryan entered the kitchen and set Kenzie's meal down. He'd texted her again around seven to see if things had slowed down at all. It'd taken her twenty minutes to respond, and she'd told him it was still as busy as when she arrived. Since she'd specifically told him not to rush home, he'd stayed at the pub until about a quarter past eight. But even if she hadn't been able to get a head start on her end-of-the-night responsibilities, she should be home now. Pulling up his contact list, Ryan dialed Kenzie's number as he headed downstairs to let Marley out of the laundry room.

"Hey, Marley." He scratched the dog behind his ear as he waited for Kenzie to answer. Instead, it rang several times before switching over to her voice mail.

He didn't bother to leave a message. Unless she was with a patient and couldn't get to her phone, Kenzie always answered. Even when she was driving, she'd answer using the vehicle's hands-free option. So the only reason he could think of to explain why she might not answer was because she was on the phone with someone else. Although in the past when that had happened, she put the other caller on hold long enough to answer and let Ryan know she'd call him back.

Opening the back door, he let the dog out and tried

Kenzie again. Like the first time, the phone rang before her voice mail picked up. This time he left a message and then sent her a text message too.

He didn't know who had been working with her tonight, but if a coworker had asked her to do something after work, Kenzie would have let him know. Not only that, she'd be answering her phone.

It seemed like a long shot, but while he waited for Marley to finish up outside, he found the number for Parkview. On the off chance something was wrong with her phone and she was still at work, hopefully she'd answer.

"You have reached Parkview Immediate Care. The office is currently closed. If this is a medical emergency, please go to the nearest emergency room. If this is not an emergency and you wish to…," the recording began. He didn't bother to listen to the rest of the message.

A vision of Kenzie's car mangled with her trapped inside turned his blood to ice. Occasionally drivers swerved to avoid animals and ended up running off the road and into trees. He'd read a story about a month ago about a teenage girl whose car flipped on a rural road and went into a heavily wooded area. She ended up being trapped there for thirty-six hours before two local hunters found her. Kenzie's commute didn't take her through any secluded areas, but that didn't rule out the possibility of an accident.

Grabbing his keys, he let the dog back inside. "Marley, I'll be back."

He picked the most direct route to the clinic. Since the chance of heavy traffic was slim at this time of night, it seemed like the most likely route Kenzie would have taken home. Keeping his speed well under the limit, he looked for Kenzie's car or any sign of a recent accident. Other than a cop who'd pulled over a motorist about two miles from Parkview, nothing caught his attention.

Except for the illuminated sign, the immediate care clinic was in complete darkness and there were no cars around. Pulling into the parking lot, he drove around to the back of the building where employees parked, and his heart stopped. Like the lot in the front, this one was empty too. If Kenzie's car was gone, she'd left work.

"Where the hell are you?" Again his thoughts went back to a car accident. If Kenzie was at an emergency room and unable to communicate with the staff, they wouldn't contact him, since he wasn't a relative. The authorities might have contacted her parents.

He didn't have either of her parents' phone numbers, but he knew who could get them for him. Lyle Cardi, one of the geniuses who worked in the cyber division, spent more time at the office than he did at home. If on the rare chance he wasn't already at Elite Force, the guy lived closer to the office than anyone else in the division.

His coworker answered on the second ring.

"Hey, Lyle. I need some help," Ryan greeted before he explained the situation. "Can you get me the phone numbers for Edward and Maeve Armstrong? They live somewhere in Springfield. And I need you to get a location on Kenzie's cell." Fingers crossed it was still on and in her possession.

"I'm already at the office working on a project. I'll call you when I have the numbers."

Although he didn't expect an answer, Ryan tried Kenzie's phone a third time, but like his first two attempts, all he got was her voice mail. Under certain circumstances, he could sit around all day and wait for information. Tonight wasn't one of those times. While Lyle worked on getting him the numbers and hopefully finding Kenzie's phone, he needed to do something. A random drive around the area looking for signs of an accident most likely wouldn't accomplish anything. The emergency room at Winchester Memorial probably wouldn't give him any information either if he called, since he wasn't Kenzie's next of kin. So until he had the information from Lyle, he had little choice but to head back to Kenzie's house and pray she showed up.

His phone rang before the garage door finished closing behind him.

Please be Kenzie. Instead, Lyle's name and number stared back at him when he picked up the phone.

"Hey, Salty, I got the phone numbers and the couple's home address," Lyle said. "I haven't located Kenzie's cell phone yet. I'll keep working on triangulating its last position, but I figured you'd want these now."

When he'd left, Ryan hadn't bothered to turn off the lights or put Marley back in his room again. Usually after being alone for several hours, the dog wanted attention. Tonight, he walked past Ryan and parked his butt near the door, as if waiting for Kenzie to come home too. *Yeah, I'm working on it, buddy.*

Grabbing a sheet of paper off the notepad she kept on the refrigerator, Ryan jotted down the numbers and both addresses. "Thanks for your help. Call me when you find her cell." He disconnected the call before Lyle could reply and punched in Edward's phone number.

Despite it being after nine o'clock, Kenzie's father answered right away.

"Ed, it's Ryan. Have you heard from Kenzie?" Ryan didn't bother with a proper greeting.

"Uh, no. I haven't talked to her today. Why?"

What he had to tell him, no parent ever wanted to hear, but Edward and Maeve needed to know something was wrong. "She's not home. I drove by the clinic and her car isn't there. I've tried calling her, and she's not answering."

"She's friendly with some of her coworkers. Maybe they went out for a drink or a late dinner." The slight tremor in

Edward's voice was almost inaudible, but Ryan picked up on it.

Ryan didn't know the exact response he expected, but that sure as hell wasn't it. In Armstrong's shoes, he'd be hanging up the phone and calling the police. Rubbing the back of his neck, he wondered why Kenzie's father wasn't doing that instead of coming up with bullshit excuses that didn't make any sense.

"Kenzie knew I'd be at her house waiting for her. She would have called if she went out with friends. Something is wrong." Her father might not feel any need to do anything, but it would not stop him. "A buddy of mine is working on getting the location of her cell. While I wait to hear back from him, I'm going to call the police."

"Don't call the police."

He'd never heard anyone sound more desperate than Kenzie's father. Edward knew something.

"Why the hell not?" Unless the guy started explaining fast, this conversation was over, because he needed to find her. "Unless you know where Kenzie is, she's missing."

"I don't know where she is, Ryan."

He'd been working with guys like Armstrong for eight years. Men like him didn't let fear overtake them. They shoved it in a lockbox and left it there. Right now, fear had control over Kenzie's dad. Ryan could hear it in every word he uttered.

"But the same person who took my wife has Kenzie. If I get the police involved, he promised to kill them. He sent me pictures of them. I'm waiting for him to contact me again with instructions."

Ryan's ability to form words stopped, and graphic images of abused and tortured women assaulted him.

"Ryan?" Edward's voice pulled him back. "Please don't call the police. Let me handle this."

He didn't know who the kidnapper was or what his ultimate goal was, but Edward couldn't handle it himself. Even if he could, Ryan wouldn't let him. Not when it involved Kenzie's life.

"Even if you do what this guy wants, it's unlikely he'll let Kenzie and your wife go. We both know that." One call to Ax, and he'd have HRT and Elite Force's other resources at his disposal. "I won't call the police, but I'm going to get Elite Force involved. Do you think anyone is watching your house?" If someone had eyes on Ed's house to make sure he didn't go to the police, Ryan didn't want them to follow Kenzie's father to Elite Force's headquarters either.

"I haven't seen anyone suspicious, but it's possible. If I wanted to make sure someone didn't go to the police, I'd have eyes on them at all times."

Yeah, he would too. "When I get to work, I'll set up a video conference between you and the team."

SEVENTEEN

Some people were afraid to die. Kenzie wasn't. She never had been. Death was simply a part of life. When she died, though, she didn't want it to be painful. She wanted to go to sleep one night and not wake up again. She didn't know what her kidnappers had planned, but she doubted her death would be painless. If it wasn't painless, she prayed it was at least quick, not some long, drawn-out affair.

The SUV hit another rut in the road, and Kenzie pitched forward. They'd been driving for some time now. At first, the road had been fairly smooth, and they didn't stop, suggesting they were traveling on a highway. After a while, the speed seemed to slow down, and the SUV made occasional stops as if they'd approached a traffic light or stop sign, making her believe they'd exited the highway and were driving through a city or town. The road they were driving on now was not well maintained, and every bump they hit only made her motion sickness worse. Honestly, she didn't know how she'd managed not to puke.

It took some effort, but she got herself back onto her side

instead of her face as the vehicle stopped briefly before it continued forward slowly. For the first time in what seemed like forever, some light shone in through the heavily tinted windows. The driver turned off the ignition, and then she heard what sounded like a garage door closing.

The vehicle's door slammed shut, and she waited for the kidnappers to get her. With her hands and ankles bound, she didn't stand a chance of escaping. At some point, though, they might untie her, and if they did, she needed to be ready to do something. Exactly what, she had no friggin' idea, but she would not let them rape and murder her without putting up a fight.

Florescent light flooded the trunk when the liftgate went up, nearly blinding her, and Kenzie blinked several times. Without saying a word, the same guy who'd broken into her house lifted her out of the trunk.

Kenzie scanned her surroundings. They were inside a large garage, the type attached to a home. A van was parked next to the vehicle she'd arrived in, and there was room for one more car. A workbench littered with cans of paint and what looked like various car parts spanned the longest wall. Brown pegboards similar to the ones her dad used to hang some of his tools were mounted over the workbench, but unlike her dad's, these were empty. On the farthest wall stood a metal tool chest at least five feet tall. All the drawers were open, as if someone had been in a hurry the last time they went through it. From here she couldn't tell if there was anything inside, but if she somehow managed to get free and into the garage, the tool chest seemed like the only place where she might find something to use as a weapon. Along the same wall where the tool chest was there was a door and a staircase leading up. The guy carrying her didn't take Kenzie toward either. Instead, he carried her toward the door on their left and into a kitchen.

Kenzie enjoyed watching home renovation shows. Her favorite was one in which the hosts took old homes, sometimes even ones abandoned for years, and transformed them into gorgeous masterpieces. If the kitchen was a good representation of the rest of this house, it would be a prime candidate for the show. Three exposed bulbs in the ceiling lit up the room. Whatever glass shade that had once covered them was long gone. Several of the cabinet doors were missing. Both the stove and the refrigerator looked like something out of the 1950s. If someone lived here, they must eat standing up, because there wasn't so much as a stool in the room.

As if she didn't weigh more than a toddler, the man continued down a short hallway, opened a door, and went down a flight of stairs to an unfinished basement.

Similar to in the garage, cold florescent lights hung from the ceiling. A woman sat tied to a chair against the wall. She had her head down and her hair hung loose, covering the side of her face. When they reached the bottom step and it creaked, she looked up.

"Kenzie! Oh God. No," her mom shouted as she started tugging at the restraints holding her down.

Another man jogged down the steps and pulled a chair over next to her mom. He wasn't the same one who'd driven them here. Kenzie guessed he'd kidnapped her mom.

"I promised you'd have company, Maeve," the new addition to the scene said as he reached for the rope on the ground. "Hold her, Jax, and I'll tie her down."

Jax deposited her into the chair, then put one knee on top of her thighs and his hands on her shoulders, making it impossible to move.

"Do what you want with me, but let her go," Maeve demanded as she continued to struggle against her restraints.

"Sorry, we can't do that," the guy securing Kenzie to the

chair answered. "But don't worry, we won't hurt you." The rope bit into her chest as he pulled it tighter.

Jax laughed sarcastically and released her shoulders. "Shawn's right. You have nothing to worry about from us."

Shawn untied the gag and dropped it in her lap. "There's no one around but us, so if you scream, it won't do you any good. But I don't want to hear it. Keep quiet and I won't put it back."

How many did "us" consist of? And if these clowns didn't plan to hurt them, who did?

In the movies, kidnapping victims sometimes managed to move whatever object they were tied to, cut their ropes, and escape. Even if Kenzie could move the chair, there wasn't anything useful around her.

"Are you okay? Did they hurt you?" her mom asked once they were alone.

"I've lost all feeling in my hands and feet, but otherwise I'm okay. You?" Other than the bruise on her mom's cheek, she looked okay, but her mom would have put up a fight when they took her.

"I think I broke my wrist."

"Do you any idea of what is going on?" Kenzie didn't live in a bubble. She knew men kidnapped random women. Sometimes they kept them hostage for years. Other times they used them and then killed them. This wasn't a random kidnapping. It couldn't be, since her mom was tied to the chair next to her.

Maeve shook her head. "On the ride here I heard one of them make a call. He said 'it is done.' By now your dad must have called the police."

"Ryan probably did too. He's been staying with me since what I thought was a break-in attempt."

"Why didn't you me tell about that?" her mom asked, sounding concerned.

If she could move her shoulders, Kenzie would've

shrugged. "Ryan was there when it happened, and the guy ran away. The police assumed it was the same punk who broke into another house in the neighborhood the week before. Turns out it was Jax."

"Then whoever the guys upstairs are waiting for has had this planned for a while."

She'd reached the same conclusion. "This has to have something to do with Dad, maybe one of his old cases. It's the only thing that makes sense."

There might have been a few kids in high school who didn't like her, but Kenzie didn't have enemies. The same was true of her mom. Everyone loved her. Her dad, on the other hand, was a different story. Although he'd only been doing his job, there were probably a lot of people he'd sent to prison during his career who hated him. Kidnapping a man's wife and daughter would be a great way to get revenge.

Overhead, she heard footsteps, and she held her breath as she glanced at the stairs. It'd been clear when Shawn and Jax claimed they wouldn't hurt her and her mom that there was someone who would. Had the individual arrived or had one of the creeps upstairs gotten up to use the bathroom?

When several seconds passed and no one appeared, she closed her eyes and sighed. The longer they stayed tied up here alone and unharmed, the more time the police had to find them. "How many do you think are upstairs?"

"Shawn had a partner, so unless he left after he dropped us off, there must be at least three."

"Jax wasn't alone either, and there was a van in the garage when I got here," Kenzie said.

Ryan set a record getting from Kenzie's house to Elite Force Headquarters. When he pulled into his usual spot in the employee parking lot, he found both Spike and Keith exiting their vehicles. No one said a word as they headed inside the building and up to the fourth floor, the home to both the firm's cyber division and the Hostile Response Team.

Now that the videoconference with Edward was live and Ax, as well as the available members of the team, were gathered in the team's meeting room, it was time to get some answers. The first one being who the hell had Kenzie and her mom.

The team's meeting room was Ax's domain. He asked the questions and gave the orders. Tonight wasn't any different. "Mr. Armstrong, do you know who has your daughter and wife?"

The man that appeared on the flat-screen wasn't the friendly father Ryan ate dinner with a few weekends ago. He also wasn't the approachable, not-a-hair-out-of-place firearms instructor Ryan had at the academy. Edward's hair stood up in every direction as if lightning had struck him, and he kept cracking his knuckles. Cold, determined eyes stared out from behind glasses. A few times while they'd waited for the rest of the team, Ryan saw fear in the other man's eyes. It was the same fear Ryan was fighting to keep locked away until Kenzie and her mom were safe.

"Call me Ed," he said, rubbing his forehead as if in pain. "Yes. Gabriel Wilson."

A name didn't tell him where the two women were, but it was more than he'd had when he walked in the building.

Ed cracked three of the fingers on his left hand as he continued. "I arrested him about four years ago. It was one of the last cases I worked before I retired."

"Was he convicted?" Ax asked. Not every arrest led to a guilty verdict and a prison sentence.

"Yeah. He got two to four years."

"What did you arrest him for?" Ax asked the same question Ryan wanted to. The FBI investigated a diverse list of crimes. If they knew what the government had gotten Gabriel Wilson for, they'd have a better idea of the kind of person they were dealing with.

"Insider trading. He hacked into the computers of Jeanine Burr, the CEO of Sagewood Technologies, and used the information he obtained to invest. I always suspected he did it to other companies too, but I couldn't prove it."

A guy who spent his time hacking into computers didn't sound like someone who'd resort to kidnapping, so clearly this wasn't your typical hacker.

Under normal circumstances, he'd leave the questions to Ax. Tonight Ryan couldn't do that. This wasn't just another assignment. "What else can you tell us? Does he have any family members in the area?" There might be a dozen Gabriel Wilsons living in the state, and that was assuming he lived in Virginia. The more they knew about the guy, the quicker they might track him down.

"When I investigated him, he was living in Hillsboro with his wife and two children. But the wife filed for divorce around the same time the case went to trial. He also had family in Norfolk, including a younger brother."

Statistically, computer hackers weren't violent. They much preferred to do damage using their keyboards instead of with guns. If Wilson had resorted to violence now, there was a good chance he'd done it before tonight.

"Does he have a history of violence?" Ryan asked.

Kenzie's dad cracked the knuckles on his other hand. "He had no prior arrests. Several people I interviewed at the time said he had a temper. But others described him as a devoted family guy."

Yeah, anyone that kidnaps another person is a real family guy.

Ax continued to ask Edward questions that might help

them locate Wilson, until the phone on the conference table rang. His expression gave nothing away as he listened to the caller and jotted something down on a notepad. "Find out everything you can about a Gabriel C. Wilson, last known address in Hillsboro. The FBI arrested him about four years ago. And see if he has any family still living in the state." He put the receiver down and turned in Ryan's direction. "Lyle got a general location for Kenzie's cell phone."

Unless they were the dumbest criminals in history, Kenzie wouldn't be anywhere near the device. If the team found the phone, though, they might find clues to help them track her down.

Edward looked about ready to speak when a phone in the room with him rang. Shifting in his chair, Kenzie's father picked up his cell phone and looked at the screen. "It's the same number Wilson called me from before," he said, thumbing on the device.

Ryan stopped breathing and focused on the half of the conversation he could hear and Edward's face. Once again he saw determination slip from the man's eyes and fear replace it.

"I understand," Kenzie's father said. "I'll be there." Raking his fingers through his hair, Edward ended the call and put the phone down. "I'm supposed to be at Alexandria Station in twenty minutes. Once I'm there, Wilson will contact me again with more instructions."

"Good, that gives us a little breathing room," Ax said, as if reading Ryan's thoughts. Edward might not be in the city, but the team was, so they could get to the station before Kenzie's father arrived. "Neil, get your gear and get over to the train station. I want you inside before Ed arrives. Matt and Thad, you're on surveillance outside the station," Ax continued as he began giving out orders. "Keith, get the chopper ready so we can go as soon as we get a location."

Ryan never realized how long twenty minutes could be. Once Ax finished giving out assignments, he'd gotten his gear together. As soon as they had a location, Keith would fly the rest of the team in. But first, they needed a location. Until they had it, all he could do was wait. Seated at the conference table, he listened to the audio feeds coming in.

"Armstrong just left the parking garage, and he's headed for the entrance." Matt's voice came through the speaker. He was positioned across the street from the station's parking garage, while Thad sat in a car across from the main entrance.

"I've got eyes on him," Neil informed them all. "He's answering his cell phone."

Silence followed Neil's comment, and Ryan stared at the speaker as if doing so would magically make it spew useful information.

"He opened a locker and removed a bag." Neil finally spoke again.

"Did he take anything out of it?" Ax asked.

"Not yet," Neil answered. "But his call with Wilson ended and he put his cell phone in the locker. Wilson must have left him a burner to use."

Wilson might be a sick son of a bitch, but he wasn't a dummy.

"Thad, he's headed toward the main exit," Neil said.

"Got him," Thad replied.

Whatever you do, don't lose him. Eventually, Wilson would lead Edward to his location. Hopefully, it would be the same place the women were being held. Regardless, with his cell safely locked away at the station, physically tailing Edward was the only way to know where he was. If they lost sight of him, they'd lose their only way of finding Kenzie and her mom.

When he'd been putting together his plan, Gabe had briefly considered meeting Armstrong at the train station and driving him out to the house. The sooner he had the guy, the sooner he could kill Armstrong's family and finally him. But he wanted the guy to suffer as much as possible. Every minute the former agent knew Gabe had his wife and daughter but wasn't able to get to them was another minute of torture for the guy.

By now Armstrong should be back in his car. Punching in the number for the disposable phone he'd left in the locker, Gabe waited for him to pick up. He didn't have to wait long.

"Where am I meeting you?" Armstrong asked.

The guy's clear and calm voice enraged him. Gabe had the guy's wife and daughter. At this moment, anything could be happening to them. The man shouldn't sound calm.

"Go to Civic Center Park in Rockville. At this time of night, you should be able to get there in about thirty minutes. I know you want to keep your wife and daughter safe, so you won't call the police. But just to make sure you don't slip and call them, I think we'll use this time to catch up." He'd already told Armstrong what would happen if the police got involved, but it didn't hurt to remind him not to try anything. So far everything was going as he'd planned; he wanted to keep it that way.

"You never told me you had a daughter, Ed. Kenzie's beautiful, by the way. She looks a lot like her mom, except for her eyes. They are quite a unique color. When she treated me at the clinic, I couldn't stop looking at them." He wanted the man to know he'd been close enough to his daughter to determine the color of her eyes. "You might remember I have a daughter and a son. They're living in Denver now with my ex-wife. How long have you and Maeve been married? I understand she retired from the FBI too and now spends her time photographing weddings."

Gabe smiled as he imagined the former agent's face. No one liked a stranger knowing so much about the people they loved. A man like Armstrong would hate it even more than most. This was going to be one of the most enjoyable conversations he'd had in a long time.

EIGHTEEN

As Ryan expected, Kenzie was no longer in possession of her cell phone. Alex found it, as well as Kenzie's car with the keys, on the ground in a wooded area about fifteen minutes from Parkview Immediate Care and within a short drive to the highway. Although Alex was on her way back to the firm with the fingerprints she'd collected, Ryan wasn't optimistic they'd get anything useful. So far Gabriel Wilson's plan had been well thought out and executed. If he'd grabbed Kenzie himself, he wouldn't have made the mistake of leaving fingerprints behind in her car. If he'd hired guys to do it for him, he would have picked men who knew what they were doing. Either way, whatever fingerprints Alex lifted probably belonged to Kenzie and any friends she'd had in the car recently.

Locating the phone and car hadn't been a complete waste of time. Alex had found no blood anywhere in the vehicle. Although it didn't guarantee Kenzie hadn't been injured, the lack of blood gave him hope. She also found two sets of footprints, both too large to belong to Kenzie, near the vehicle, so whoever had taken her wasn't working alone.

"I lost him. Does anyone see him?" Thad's voice came through the speaker, and Ryan's heart stopped beating.

They'd followed Edward from the train station to Civic Center Park. At that time of night, the place was deserted, making it almost impossible to conceal their vehicles while at the same time keeping at least one set of eyes on Armstrong at all times. Thad had managed it until Ed got out of his car and started walking. If they lost a visual on Kenzie's father, they had no other way of tracking him.

"Nothing here," Matt replied.

"Neil?" Ax asked.

"A silver two-door sedan is exiting the park. There are at least two people inside," Neil answered.

"Stay with it until you determine whether or not Ed's in the car." Ax drummed his fingers on the table as he spoke. "Thad—"

"I think I know where Gabriel Wilson is keeping Kenzie and her mom." Mad Dog, who'd been over helping cyber learn everything they could about Wilson, entered the room holding a laptop. "We traced him back to Merit Consolidated. It's a shell corporation. Somehow the FBI missed it. About five months ago, Merit bought an old estate with twenty-five acres of land in Thurmont, Maryland. It's less than an hour from the park in Rockville to the estate."

If he'd kidnapped someone, a secluded estate no one knew he owned with twenty-five acres of land would be the type of place he'd want to hold them.

"If Wilson is going there, Keith can get the team there before he arrives," Mad Dog continued.

He didn't know if Wilson had anyone with the women or not. If the place was so secluded, he might have decided it wasn't necessary. Either way, if the team got there first, they'd have the upper hand when Wilson and Ed arrived.

"The car merged onto Interstate 270 North," Neil said, giving them an update. "It's Armstrong in the car."

"Assuming the estate is his destination, 270 North would be the most direct route," Mad Dog commented, further convincing Ryan that Wilson was going to Thurmont. It must have done the same for Ax.

Ryan was already out of his chair when Ax commanded them to go.

Although his mom was religious and had dragged him and his siblings to church every Sunday, he'd never believed in prayers or good luck. Now as the chopper lifted off, he prayed they got Kenzie and her mom out safely.

Located a good mile from the road, the house looked as though someone had dropped it in the middle of nowhere. Except for a small clearing in front and a much larger one behind it, trees surrounded the place, providing the owner with plenty of privacy. From the chopper, he didn't see any vehicles parked outside, but what looked like a garage extended from one side of the building.

"How do you want to handle this?" Keith's voice came over Ryan's headset.

If they lingered too long in one spot, the noise might make someone inside curious. "We need to know how many are inside." Unless left with no other option, you never wanted to go into a potentially hostile situation without knowing what you were up against.

"I should be able to make one low pass," Keith answered.

When its employees went into the field, Elite Force Security made sure they had access to whatever technology they needed. The Forward-looking Infrared or FLIR camera mounted to the chopper would pick up the body heat of anyone in the house. So while it wouldn't tell them which ones were Kenzie and her mom, the team would at least know where everyone was in the building, allowing them to formulate a plan. It'd also let them know if they'd been wrong and there wasn't anyone in the house.

Six distinct heat signatures appeared on the video monitor secured to the ceiling of the chopper. There were four of them clustered on one level, while the other two were close to each other. There was no way of being 100 percent certain, but Ryan's gut told him the two located close together were Kenzie and her mom.

"Looks like four hostiles," he informed the team, a plan already forming in his head as Keith veered off.

They cut through the woods and approached the sprawling house. Light spilled out of two rooms on the main level and from one of the basement windows. The entire second floor remained dark. As they'd planned, Ryan, Spike, and Mad Dog got into position at the front of the house while James, Christian, and Connor circled around the back.

On assignments, Ryan always managed to distance his emotions from what he had to do. Tonight he was having a difficult time doing that. He recognized that putting a bullet into each of the hostiles heads was wrong. Yet it still appealed to him. And if he got in there and discovered any of them had done more than hold Kenzie and her mom against their will, what was right and wrong might not matter anymore.

"Now." On his order, everything happened at once. James and Spike sent flash grenades through the two windows where there was light. Ryan breached the front door, while Christian took care of the back one.

Neither Jax nor Shawn had come downstairs since they tied Kenzie to the chair. She knew they hadn't left, because occasionally she'd hear footsteps above them. Every time she did, she wondered if the person they were working with had arrived.

A low rumble of thunder penetrated the silence.

"I think it's thundering out," her mom said, speaking for the first time in several minutes. "Twix hates when it thunders."

The only dog she knew more afraid of thunderstorms than her parents' was Marley. His anxiety vest was the only thing that ever seemed to help him during storms. Even if Ryan was at her house waiting to hear something from the police, he wouldn't know to put it on him. "Hopefully it'll be a short storm." Another rumble of thunder rolled through the room. "Ryan wants me to have Thanksgiving with him and his family." Considering their circumstances, it was a ridiculous statement, but they needed something to focus on besides the fact they might both die tonight. "You and Dad won't mind if I go, will you?" Kenzie asked as she tried to ignore the itch on her thigh. Really, as if she didn't have enough problems, now she had an itch she couldn't scratch.

"Of course not. Things between you two must be serious if he wants you to meet his family."

Boom. Boom. It sounded like small bombs were exploding in the house.

Kenzie saw her mom's lips moving, but she couldn't hear her voice over the ringing in her ears. She wasn't an expert in lip reading, but she thought her mom said, "That wasn't thunder." Kenzie agreed.

Dust sprinkled down from the ceiling, and Kenzie thought she heard footsteps pounding across the floor above them.

Bang. Even over the ringing in her ears, Kenzie recognized the sound. She'd been to the range enough times with her dad. Some company had arrived, and it wasn't welcome. Another gun fired, and Kenzie mentally crossed her fingers, since doing so physically was impossible.

Be the police. Criminals went after other criminals. Whoever had busted their way in upstairs might be after

Shawn and his buddies. If they were, God knew what it meant for her and her mom.

Additional light spilled down the stairs when someone opened the basement door. Blood roared in her ears, and she balled her bound hands into tight fists. Large black boots came into view before their owner did. Was Jax or Shawn on their way down, or was it their recent company?

Ryan! Dressed all in black, including his bulletproof vest, Ryan approached them with his gun drawn. Kenzie blinked while her brain processed the vision in front of her, and then whatever self-preservation mechanism had kept her from losing it broke. Tremors racked her body, and tears coursed down her face.

Kneeling in front of her, Ryan pulled a knife from a sheath clipped to his belt and cut through the rope around her feet. "Kenz, it's okay." He cupped her face and met her eyes. "You're both safe." Ryan walked behind her and first cut through the ropes securing her to the chair and then through the restraints binding her wrists. Once she was free, he cut through Maeve's bindings.

"We need to get out of here before Wilson and your dad arrive. Can you walk?" he asked.

Later, she could fall apart when she and everyone she cared about were safely away from this place. Nodding, she took in a deep breath and wiped the tears off her cheek. "Yes." Or at least she hoped so. At the moment, her feet had the worst case of pins and needles humanly possible. When she stood, pain shot through her feet, but Kenzie ignored it.

"What about you, Maeve?" Ryan asked.

Next to her, her mom struggled to get her emotions under control, and judging by the way her hands shook, she wasn't having a lot of luck, but she nodded. "I can do whatever you need me to."

Questions swirled in Kenzie's head, but right now she

only wanted an answer to one. The rest could wait until later. "Is Dad okay?" If Ryan wanted to get them out of here before Wilson arrived, he wasn't a friend helping her dad find them.

Ryan paused on the top step and glanced back at her. "Yeah."

She heard the unspoken part of his sentence. Her dad was okay, but he might not stay that way.

It didn't appear as though whatever had caused the boom damaged the house. As Ryan led her and her mom toward the back door, she kept an eye out for Shawn, Jax, and his friends. Except for the discarded food containers and the sound of the television coming from down the hall, there was no evidence anyone else had been in the house.

"What happened to the jerks that were here?" she asked.

"They're nice and comfortable with Christian keeping them company until we can hand them off to the police."

Ryan's answer explained the lack of a police presence when they walked outside. Not only weren't there any police cruisers surrounding the house, but there weren't any vehicles at all unless you counted the helicopter parked in the backyard.

"I need the two of you to go with Keith," Ryan shouted so they could hear him over the noise of the helicopter.

She'd rather stick around and make sure her dad remained safe. She didn't need to ask her mom to know she felt the same way. But doing so would only mean Ryan and whoever else was with him had more to worry about than getting her dad to safety.

After all the sweating she'd done while locked first in the trunk and then in the basement, she probably smelled like an old gym bag. She didn't care. Before Ryan went into yet another potentially dangerous situation, she was going to hug him and tell him what she'd been meaning to tell him for days. With his bulletproof vest on, hugging Ryan was a little like hugging a wall. "I love you. Please be careful."

He kept his arms loose around her and brushed his lips against her forehead. "Love you too. Don't worry about anything."

———

He hadn't specifically been looking for a place to dump three bodies when he found the listing. Instead, he'd been searching for a place away from everyone and everything. A house he could go to on the weekends. When he looked at the run-down estate in the middle of nowhere though, he'd known it was exactly what he needed so that no one would ever find the bodies of Edward Armstrong, his wife, and any children he might have.

Gabe's left knee bounced up and down. With each mile they'd driven, his anticipation had grown. Now with his house mere moments away, excitement threatened to make him rush, something he didn't want to do. He wanted to draw out Edward Armstrong's suffering as long as humanly possible.

His mind remained focused on the various possibilities as he turned onto the dirt driveway. Years of neglect and the weather had done a job on it. Eventually, he'd have the thing paved, but not until they tore down the current structure and built his new home. If everything went as planned, work would start next spring.

"I told the guys to leave Kenzie and Maeve alone." Even after Gabe had Armstrong in his car, his hands first bound together with nylon restraints and then also bound to the car door, he'd kept talking to the man. For the most part, it had been a one-sided conversation, but he didn't mind. Even when Armstrong didn't comment, Gabe knew he had to be getting under the guy's skin. "They probably listened."

Despite his attempts to get Armstrong angry, the guy remained quiet. Gabe couldn't resist glancing over at his passenger. The former FBI agent kept his eyes focused straight ahead and his hands clenched into fists.

After rounding a curve, the small excavator he'd bought came into view. If he dumped the Armstrongs somewhere in the woods, he ran the risk of an animal finding them and carrying a body part off. Burying them eight feet underground required more work but provided him with greater security. The excavator had made digging the Armstrongs' new home easy. Now that he owned the machine, who knew what uses he might have for it after they finished his new house.

Unlike with a lot of homes, the garage was the first thing you got a good look at when you approached the structure. The plans his architect was working on changed that. If anyone visited, they would see the front of the house and have to drive around the side to reach the garage.

The vehicle's headlights lit up the front of the garage. "You're the one I want. Keep cooperating, and your family will be on their way home soon just like I promised." The previous owners had done very little to keep the house up to date, yet they had at some point installed an automatic garage door.

Hitting the button, he waited for the door to go up. Unlike the last time he'd been out here, nothing happened. "Damn it."

He'd never been a gun guy like his brother. Xander had a nice collection of both handguns and hunting rifles. Not long after his release from prison, Xander took him on a hunting trip in South Carolina. Since then, he'd gone to the range many times with his brother and became very competent with firearms.

Gabe put the car in park and pointed his 9mm at Armstrong. "I'll be right back." According to the forecast, the rain would not start until after sunrise. Once again the meteorologists were wrong. As Gabe walked toward the garage door, a light rain started.

Before he grabbed the handle, the garage door flew up, and he found himself facing four armed men. Immediately, Gabe raised his gun.

"Drop it," one of the dudes in front of him shouted as Gabe squeezed the trigger.

Excruciating pain ripped through his right chest, and he stumbled backward before hitting the ground. Something warm covered his chest. Blood.

Armstrong should be the one bleeding all over the ground right now, not him. He'd spent so much time planning everything out. This shouldn't be happening.

Visions of Ava and Logan formed. His chances of ever seeing them again weren't great, but as long as he lived it remained a possibility. If he didn't get some help, he'd die. The rain started to fall harder, pelting his skin. Black spots appeared before his eyes.

A bag or something hit the ground near his head. Hands tore open his shirt and more pain sliced through his body as the owner of the hands applied pressure to the wound.

"ETA on paramedics is five minutes, Connor," someone said.

It was the last thing Gabe heard before he lost consciousness.

NINETEEN

Kenzie had always wanted to go for a ride in a helicopter. In her head, she'd pictured flying over Hawaii, one of the many places on her bucket list to visit, and getting a bird's-eye view of the islands. Instead, her first flight occurred because she needed to get away from a run-down house where some creeps had held her and her mom captive before her dad and a nutcase named Wilson arrived.

Keith gave them just enough time to get seated before he lifted off. Kenzie wasn't sure how far they traveled, but when he landed, paramedics and police officers greeted her and her mom. Keith left as the paramedics helped them get settled in the ambulance and then the police escorted them to a local hospital.

Although they both claimed to be fine, the doctors in the emergency room insisted on examining them before allowing the police to question them. Other than some bruising on her wrists from the ropes and on her knees from when Jax tackled her to the ground, Kenzie was physically fine. Emotionally... well, that was another story. One she'd tackle later. As her mom suspected, she had broken her wrist, but compared to the injuries they could have sustained, it wasn't a big deal.

Once the doctors gave them the okay, the police descended on them, wanting a thorough retelling of the night's events, starting with when the kidnappers snatched each of them. Alexandra Thompson arrived before Kenzie could get started. She introduced herself as an employee of Elite Force Security who was there to stay with Kenzie and her mom until the doctors cleared them to leave and then to escort them home. But Kenzie knew Alex didn't spend her days answering the phone or sending out invoices to customers.

Even now that they were safely at Kenzie's house, Alex remained. Truthfully, she was glad the woman was there. She didn't need to ask her mom to know she felt the same way. Sure, she'd told Alex it was okay if she wanted to leave because it seemed like the right thing to do, but deep down, Kenzie wanted her to stay. Any other time she'd feel safe behind locked doors. Tonight, she wanted an armed guard who knew what she was doing.

When her mom became anxious, she liked to snack. Unfortunately, it was a trait Kenzie shared. So while Kenzie sipped her second cup of chamomile tea, she searched for the package of double chocolate chip cookies she knew she had. Usually, she drank chamomile because she enjoyed the taste. Tonight she hoped it would help her relax as the box claimed. She wasn't holding out much hope.

Unable to find the package she wanted, Kenzie settled on the oatmeal cookies instead and headed back to the living room.

"Alex is calling Ax for an update." Kenzie handed her mom the package of cookies. It seemed like an eternity since they'd left Ryan and the rest of his team to wait for someone named Wilson and her dad. In reality, she knew it'd only been a couple of hours at most.

Her mom didn't waste any time ripping the package open. "I'm sure everything is fine." Her optimistic words didn't match her tone.

She kept telling herself the same thing. Until her dad and Ryan both walked in the door, her brain refused to stop playing various scenarios, all with deadly outcomes. She had no intention of sharing the truth with her mom though. "Yeah, I know. Do you have any idea who Wilson is?"

Her mom shook her head as she sipped her tea. "The name doesn't ring any bells, but unless it somehow involved me, your dad never gave me specifics of any case."

True. When she'd lived at home, occasionally her dad would mention he'd arrested someone or that one of his cases was finally going to trial, but he never mentioned names.

"My best guess is that he's someone your dad arrested after he transferred to the office in Norfolk," her mom continued as she scratched Marley's side. The dog had stayed close since they returned home.

Kenzie didn't agree. Whoever Wilson was, he'd gone to a lot of trouble to carry out his plan. A man like that wouldn't let the fact her dad lived in another state stand in his way.

Wilson. The name nagged at her again. It'd done the same thing when she'd been talking to the police. Where had she heard it recently?

"When your dad gets here, he'll—"

When she realized why the name sounded familiar, she almost dropped her tea. "Work. That's where I remember the name from." Kenzie could picture the man. He'd come in complaining of a sore throat the same night Jax broke into her house. Wilson was a fairly common name. It could be a coincidence a man named Wilson was behind the kidnapping tonight, but her intuition didn't think so.

"Last week, a patient named Gabriel Wilson insisted on seeing me rather than Tiffany. He claimed I'd treated his daughter in the past, but I didn't recognize him." Goose bumps broke out across her skin at the idea that she might have been alone with the man behind tonight's events.

Before Kenzie could finish explaining her suspicions, Alex rejoined them. The minute Kenzie met Alex, she liked her, but much like with Ryan's coworker Maddie, she didn't understand why a woman would choose this line of work.

Alex gave Marley a pet as she walked by him and then sat on the sofa. "Ryan and Ed are on their way here."

"Were either of them hurt?" Just because they were on their way to the house didn't mean one or both of them hadn't suffered an injury. It only meant their injuries did not require they remain in the hospital.

"Ax didn't go into specifics, but I don't think so." Alex took a sip of her tea and set it on the table before grabbing a cookie.

Maybe other people would want Wilson dead. She didn't. After the hell he'd put them through, she wanted him and the guys working with him to spend the rest of their lives rotting behind bars. "What about Wilson?"

Alex dipped her cookie in her tea. Kenzie occasionally dipped cookies in milk or even hot chocolate, but she'd never dipped them in her chamomile tea. "He's in surgery, and the police took the four guys working for him into custody."

Ryan pulled in next to Alex's pink Volkswagen Beetle. When he'd put Kenzie and her mom on the chopper, he'd been torn. He knew his job was to stay with the team and finish the mission, but he'd wanted to be there for Kenzie. Knowing Alex was on her way to the hospital to meet Kenzie and then stay at the house with her and Maeve until he got there made watching Keith take off bearable. Barely.

"Ryan, thank you." Kenzie's father hadn't spoken since they left Elite Force Security. Unlike earlier when he spoke with police and then Ax, Ed's voice was thick and a little unsteady. "Kenzie and Maeve are alive because of you." He paused and cleared his throat. "I wouldn't have been able to save them alone."

How did he respond to that? "I'd do anything for Kenzie."

Ed studied him before he spoke again. "Yeah, I know you would." He opened the car door and swung one leg out. "We better go inside."

Unlocking the front door, Ryan stepped in the house. Right away, whatever conversation the women were having stopped, and three sets of eyes—well, four if you counted Marley's—turned in his direction. Although Kenzie had changed out of the purple scrubs she'd been wearing and into cotton shorts and an old Nationals T-shirt, she looked like she'd been through hell. Her mom didn't look much better. Like Kenzie, she'd changed and now wore a long nightshirt, probably one that belonged to her daughter, and she had a cast on one arm.

Ryan wasn't sure who moved faster, Edward or his wife and daughter. Either way, Edward embraced both women at the same time, and by the looks of it, if it was humanly possible, he'd never let either of them go.

Kenzie broke away from the group hug first and headed straight for him.

She gave him a quick once-over before throwing her arms around him. "Are you okay?"

He should be asking her that. "Didn't even get a scratch." After almost losing her, Ryan wanted nothing more than to pull her close and kiss her, but he didn't want to hurt her. She might not have any broken bones like her mom, but that didn't mean she'd walked away from the ordeal unscathed either. "More importantly, how are you?"

Her body brushed against his when she moved in closer. "A few bruises. Nothing a few days won't heal."

"Since you're here, Ryan, I'll go so all of you can get some sleep," Alex said, coming to her feet. "Maeve and Ed, I'll pick some clothes up for you before I come back later today."

Although all the Armstrongs looked exhausted, he expected it'd be a while before anyone went up to bed. Kenzie and most likely Maeve would want to know who'd kidnapped them and why. Ryan didn't blame them. He'd want answers too, but right now he didn't feel like sitting there while that conversation occurred. Instead, he wanted to take Kenzie upstairs, tuck her into bed, and then spend the next few hours just holding her and watching her sleep.

"Was Wilson someone you arrested?" Maeve asked once the four of them were alone.

"Yes, about four years ago," Ed answered. Although he and Maeve were seated, he kept his arm around her. "Afterward, his wife divorced him and moved out of state. She took their two children with her. He blames me. Tonight was all about revenge."

"I think he might have come into the clinic last week. Is his first name Gabriel?" Kenzie asked.

Ryan's heart dropped somewhere in the vicinity of his feet at the idea of Wilson being so close to Kenzie. "Yeah," he replied.

"Was anyone from your team hurt?" Maeve asked.

"Nope. Only Wilson was injured. I haven't gotten an update on his condition from Ax yet." After the hell he'd put Kenzie and her family through, he hoped the guy didn't make it.

Kenzie tried to stifle a yawn with little success.

"I want to know everything, but right now I think we should all get to bed and get some rest." Maeve stood up and reached for Ed's hand.

Kenzie and her dad didn't argue. Even Marley jumped off the sofa when he heard "bed" and trotted toward the stairs.

"We'll see you in the morning." Maeve stopped and kissed Kenzie on the cheek before leading her husband away.

Ryan waited until Kenzie's parents were out of sight before he spoke. "Do you want me to stay?"

"If you don't, I'll have to go home with you." Standing, she held out her hand. She didn't let go of it until they entered her bedroom.

He spotted the purple scrubs she'd worn in the trash basket when he went in the master bathroom to brush his teeth. Later, he'd offer to let her burn them in his fire pit. When he walked back in the bedroom, he expected Kenzie to be sound asleep, but while she was under the covers, her eyes remained open.

"I honestly thought we were going to die tonight," she said as he climbed into bed. "I don't know how you found us. You'll have to tell me when I'm not about to fall asleep." Kenzie snuggled against his side, one arm over his stomach, and propped herself up on an elbow. She lowered her head as if she planned to kiss him but stopped before her lips met his. "I love you."

She'd said the same thing before hopping on the chopper. But with everything else going on, his brain hadn't had time to processes the words. Now it did. Although physically impossible, it seemed like his heart was trying to explode from his chest like an alien in some sci-fi movie, and he could feel the pulse in his neck.

Reaching up, he cupped the back of her head and kissed her before speaking. "Love you too." When she didn't look about ready to pass out, he'd show her how much. "Try to get some sleep. If you need me for anything, wake me."

Rather than do what he told her and put her head down, she spoke again. "Thank you."

"No need to thank me. I'll always be here to protect you, Kenzie."

BOOKS BY CHRISTINA

*Loving The Billionaire, a novella

*The Teacher's Billionaire

*The Billionaire Playboy

*The Billionaire Princess

*The Billionaire's Best Friend

*Redeeming The Billionaire

*More Than A Billionaire

*Protecting The Billionaire

*Bidding On The Billionaire

*Falling For The Billionaire

*The Billionaire Next Door

*The Billionaire's Homecoming

*The Billionaire's Heart

+The Courage To Love

+Hometown Love

+The Playboy Next Door

+In His Kiss

+A Promise To Keep

+When Love Strikes

^Born To Protect

^His To Protect

*The Sherbrookes of Newport Series

+Love On The North Shore Series

^Elite Force Security

ABOUT THE AUTHOR

USA Today Best Selling author, Christina Tetreault started writing at the age of 10 on her grandmother's manual typewriter and never stopped. Born and raised in Lincoln, Rhode Island, she has lived in four of the six New England states since getting married in 2001. Today, she lives in New Hampshire with her husband, three daughters and two dogs. When she's not driving her daughters around to their various activities or chasing around the dogs, she is working on a story or reading a romance novel. Currently, she has three series out, The Sherbrookes of Newport, Love on The North Shore and Elite Force Security. You can visit her website http://www.christinatetreault.com or follow her on Facebook to learn more about her characters and to track her progress on current writing projects.

Printed in Great
Britain
by Amazon

31113322R00129